Varney

The

Vampyr

Book One:

The Feast of Blood

Written and Illustrated
by
David Lowrie

Acknowledgements

Writing a book, especially as this my first novel, can be a lonely place full of self-doubt and worry; and then excitement and triumph; and then back to the self-doubt.

Fortunately I was not alone when writing Varney, but had a lot of support from people who kept me going when I wasn't sure.

And so thank you to:

Jack, Emily and Daniel Furlong- who will always be my George, Flora and Henry! Thanks for enjoying the book, and walking around quoting it!,

Rebecca Furlong for supporting, art critiques and generally being a lovely sister,

My lovely daughter Emelia for proof reading the whole thing,

Rachel and Elinor Miller for their support and feedback,

Carol Thersby for your support,

Pat O'Neil, for all your suggestions,

Richie Stephens, for all your support and feedback,

Rob Hatton, for playtesting (as usual!),

Rory Thersby for some great feedback,

Simon Scott, for your excellent feedback,

Joe Cheal, for catching a few gremlins

And finally:

My wonderful family: Vanessa, Emelia and Jeannie - for supporting and encouraging me, and giving me the time to write this.

Chapter One

You know that house near you, the one at the end of the road? The one that looks a bit scary. The one you always walk by really quickly. But only walk, never run, as if you ran - he'd chase you.

But back to the house. It's an old house, set back from the road. It's thin and tall, with tall and thin windows. In the middle is a crooked green front door, paint peeling everywhere. The mortar is crumbling from between the brickwork, and the whole house smells of damp and decay.

It's partly hidden behind a high stone wall, a metal gate as the only way in. The gate is warped, with rusted and is never closed, swinging freely in the wind, banging and clanging against the gate post.

Sometimes it swings freely when there is no wind.

The garden is overgrown, with weeds up to your ears - no matter how tall you are. The long, broken path twists and turns its way from the door to the gate; and turns and twists from the gate to the door; depending on which way you are going.

It's never sunny in that garden. No flowers grow, the trees are half dead, and grey clouds seem to forever hover above the roof - even on a hot summer's day.

There's never any light at the windows, except in the top room on the third floor - and the light that is sometimes seen is a faint amber, flickering like a flame. Every now and then as you walk past you think you see out of the corner of your eye a shadowy shape pass by a window, but when you turn and look you see nothing at all.

No one comes and goes to the house.

No post is ever delivered.

No parcels ever arrive.
No visitors knock on the door.
No one is ever seen entering or leaving the house.

But the house is never up for sale, or rent. Kids never try to vandalise it, no one tries to break into it; and no one, NO ONE, visits it for trick or treating.

Somehow everyone knows, although no one knows, that it's occupied.
But occupied by who?
Or What?

Chapter Two

George sighed; the other two were late. Again. Because of that, they had now missed the school bus. As Mum was at work, this meant they'd have to take the long walk home – and the sun was already dropping below the horizon. He saw them both running out of the school gate: Flora in the lead, Henry following- as always.

"Flora, Henry, you are both late. You know the rules. You need to be here by 3:15 exactly or we miss the bus. Now we will have to walk"

"Noooo," cried Flora and Henry in unison.

"No moaning, complaining or groaning. You were late. We missed the bus. We will have to walk."

"You could have told the bus driver to wait," cried Flora

"No, Flora, I could not. The driver has a timetable to stick to, and it's unfair to make everyone else wait because you both were late. Now off we go. No more moaning, groaning or complaining remember?"

Flora and Henry stared at each other, sighed and nodded in agreement. They set off.

It wasn't a long walk home, less than a mile as they could cut through some side streets that the bus couldn't get down. However, Mum didn't like them walking so she paid for the bus.
They walked with George in the lead, followed by Flora and then Henry, who always tended to dawdle.

They were the Bannerworth kids. George was the oldest. He was nearly 11, tall and slim with thick black hair and brown eyes. George was a serious kind of boy. He loved school as he enjoyed the order and discipline of classroom. And the rules. George loved rules

Then there was Flora. She was 8 years old, with a mass of blonde-brown hair and was still waiting for her new front teeth. Flora was the night to George's day, his complete opposite as she seemed to thrive on chaos and anarchy.

Finally, there was Henry having just turned 6. He had a mop or white-blonde hair, and clear blue eyes. Henry was all too often Flora's accomplice when it came to making mischief.

They made good time, as George set a quick pace and kept shouting at Henry to keep up. The afternoon was chilling off as the last of the winter sun sunk low, casting shadows across the horizon. After about 20 minutes they were nearly home, but the worst part was still ahead. George hadn't mentioned it, and hoped the others wouldn't realise, but he had taken a slightly shorter route back home. Though it benefitted in a quicker journey, it led past The House.

They lived with their Mum in a nice, terraced house in a nice, leafy street. However, at the far end of the street was an old, dark house that was set back from the road, sitting in a garden that surrounded it like a moat. The House was on a slight hill, looming over the bottom of the street.

No one knew who lived there, but everyone thought someone did and whoever it was did not take care of The House.

The garden was overgrown like a wildflower meadow. Tall, bent trees surrounded the perimeter of the garden, just inside the tall brick wall. The trees almost seemed to reach over the wall towards passers-by, as if they were about to grab them and haul them over the wall.

All the other houses in the road were made of red brick, were tall, slender and uniform in every aspect - The House was different. It was built almost entirely of, old, dark wood, and was crooked and bent. There didn't seem to be a straight line in the house, as everything was twisted and curved. It absorbed the light looking like a dark shadow on the horizon.

"If ever there was a haunted house, it was This House," thought George.

Even Flora, who had a scant regard for her own safety, would not dare go through that gate into the garden. As they were getting close, George tried to distract them with chatter. Then they walked down the small snicket that led them right past the crooked gate.

"Err, George," said Henry, meekly "Isn't this the way past, the you know, the-"

"The House," finished Flora, glaring up at George, "I hate this house George, is scares me. Why did we come this way?"

"But it's only a hundred yards until we are on our street," said George.

This didn't help, as he may as well have said 100 chains, or 100 furlongs, or 100 barleycorns, as neither Flora nor
Henry had any idea how long 100 yards was. Then again, in England, not many people did.

"Look, just keep your heads up, your eyes open and we will soon be home," said George briskly as he marched onwards.

The other two looked at each other. Henry's little hand found its way into Flora's as she grabbed hold tight, then carrying on after George.

It seemed to last forever, the walk past the walled garden, but it took less than half a minute. They were nearly at the crooked gate, and then they would be in their own street, safe and sound. By now the sun had dipped below the horizon, and most of the street was bathed in shadow. Streetlights flickered as they started to come on in response to the lack of light, all except the ones in the snicket (which never seemed to work).

As they approached the gate, they all seemed to see a shadow out of the corner of their eyes. A seemingly impossibly tall and thin shadow. A man shaped shadow.

Then they heard a cough.

Chapter Three

They whipped around in fright, and there he was, leaning against the wide-open gate, tall and stick thin. He had a large bald head - that seemed far too big for his body. His ears were large, upswept and pointed, with the left slightly crooked. He had a long, thin face, with arched dark eyebrows, and small eyes that seemed to glowing like two red-hot coals. His skin was very pale but seemed to hold a blue hue. He had two exceptionally long yellow upper front teeth, which rested against his bottom lip.

He was dressed all in black: smart double-breasted jacket with high collars and tails at the back and a folded handkerchief in the left breast pocket. The handkerchief itself was white but seemed to be spotted with some sort of red liquid. He wore tight black trousers which made his legs look like a couple of sticks in a bin liner and on his feet were black pointed shoes that made him look like a mime. Under his jacket was a frilly white shirt, all ruffles and fluffles of a style that went out of fashion not in the last year, but in the last millennia (or the 1980s). His hands, protruding from the tight jacket arms, were long, pale, and slender, with long curved ivory fingernails - his middle finger being almost twice as long as it's fellows.

"Greetings," he said, in a voice that was both calming and exciting. It was smooth as velvet - if velvet had a voice.

"Please allow me to introduce myself."

"*Maybe,*" thought George for some reason only normally known to grown-ups, "*He's a man of wealth and taste.*"

But the strange figure continued:

"My name is Sir Francis Varney - although my friends, not that I have many, call me Frank - or Sir Francis. I am most pleased to make your acquaintance. If it is not too rude of me to ask, which of you should I eat first? I find modern table manners so confusing."

"Eat first?" asked Henry.

"Well, yesssss."

As he dragged out the word, it was like the steam hissing from a kettle. Or a snake. Or a gas leak. Probably the latter. Maybe it was due to his long front teeth.

"Well, I cannot very well eat you all at the same time now, can I? I only have one mouth."

"But why do you want to eat any of us?" enquired George.

"My mistake" said Sir Francis Varney "It is more like drink really. Poor choice of words. My humblest apologies - I feel quite embarrassed. If I could blush, I would."

"But what do you mean by drink?" asked Flora.

"My dear girl, drink your blood of course. I am sorry it is not obvious. Pale skin, pointy teeth, likes black clothes.... "

"My friend Edith likes black clothes," interrupted Henry.

"If you do not mind" said Sir Francis "I am busy here trying to drink you. This never used to happen in the 18th century. People would just scream and faint. I blame the movies and that stupid TV series about that girl with her pointy stick. Sorry, where was I. So black clothes, only out at night, does not like sunlight. Can't you tell what I am?"

"Oh - a goth? We went to Goth weekend at Whitby once "exclaimed Flora.

"No, not a goth - and thank you for reminding me of Whitby. That Vlad stole all my moves. I will never forgive him. I was around centuries before him and look who gets the fame. Not me. It is really not fair..."

The figure looked strangely sad.

"So, what are you?"

"Oh, for Go.... sorry. Cannot say that word. Is it not obvious?"

"Not really," chirped George

Sir Francis put an extremely long hand up to his face in despair, shaking his incredibly large head in disgust.

"I'm 800 years old?"

"Are you great granddad?" asked Henry. The three children stared at him pretty vacantly, which was unusual as normally they were anything but pretty vacant.

"Drinks blood? Oh please, work with me. Have your parents not let you watch dodgy horror films? The Lost Boys? Fright Night? Buffy?"

The three kids shook their heads, puzzled. Mum never watched horror films, she thought they were a bad influence. Mum preferred they watched incredibly violent revenge thrillers.

"Oh, all right, if you cannot figure it out. My name is Sir Francis Varney, and I am a vampyr."

Sir Francis felt like he was at an AA meeting when he said it aloud.

George, Henry and Flora looked at each other, and as one shouted, "COOL".

"Oh, that is not quite the reaction I usually get," said Sir Francis, looking a bit taken aback.

"So, you're a vampire?" asked George, incredulously.

"No, no, a vampyr, rhymes with ear"

"Sorry, vampyr?"

"Yesssss, that's it. Exactly right!"

"And your name is Francis Varney?" asked Flora.

"Yesssss" hissed Varney like a punctured balloon.

"And you're a vampire?"

"Vampyr. Rhymes with tier. Also, yesssss. Your point?"

"So, you're Varney the Vampire!" exclaimed Henry.

They all fell about laughing, all except Varney.

"Ok Ok , I know. It is a damned stupid name when you say it like that, but its vampyr - rhymes with deer. Please, I have told you thrice, though I can see why Dracula changed his name from Brad - he was much more popular after that. Can you not just call me Frank? Or Sir Francis? Anyway, we are now getting off topic. As I was saying, which of you shall I drink first?"

Black shadows seemed to rise around him like a cloak made from night as he lurched towards them menacingly.

They shrieked in fear.

Chapter Four

"Wait! Why should we call you anything if you are about to kill us?" called out George, standing protectively in front of the other two children.

Sir Francis was quite taken aback. His food did not normally answer back to him. He wasn't quite sure what to do.

"Well, just because I want to eat, sorry, drink you does not mean we cannot be friendly about it." said Sir Francis stopping mid lurch and looking quite puzzled.

"I'm sorry, but there's nothing friendly about you killing us. Dying can't be very nice. Was it nice for you when you died?" asked Flora pointedly.

"Well, I do not know about that," replied Sir Francis, defensively.

"Well, you are dead, aren't you? Or are you undead?" asked George.

"Oh, not you as well. It is a bit like that vampyr census. Do you identify as Dead or Undead?"

"And which are you?"

"I normally tick "prefer not to say"."

George stared at Varney in befuddlement.

"So why is there a vampire census?"

"Vampyr. Rhymes with beer. Well, we eat people, yessss?" he hissed like a punctured bike tyre.

"Drink people," George corrected "I suppose?"

"Sorry, drink. We have to be careful; if the number of vampyrs grow to the same level as the number of people, there will be a food shortage. Or a drink shortage."

"But there are about 7 billion humans. There can't be that many vampires."

"Vampyr, rhymes with here. Oh, really? That many? Wow. Then no, well not according to the last census in 1946."

"How many of you were there."

"1,764, I think."

"1,764? Is that it?"

"Well, it is not like we can have family."

"But who runs the census?" George asked. This was really his kind of thing; questions, answers, counting and working out percentages.

"Well, the Council of Vampyrs of course," Frank replied "Or is it the Vampyr Council? I always forget, and it is probably important."

"What? There's a vampire council? What do they do? Are they plotting to take over the world and rule humans?"

"Vampyr! Rhymes with mere. No, not really. They just tend to sit round a big marble table in an old castle, drinking vintage blood, and telling stories about the good old days."

"They must have some amazing stories."

"Not really."

"But you've all lived through such amazing periods in history: the renaissance, the industrial revolution, the world wars..."

"Yesssss, it all sounds remarkably interesting, but when you are there, it does not seem that way. You just tend to compare things to how they are now to back in the good old days. Do you have parent's parents?"

"You mean Grandparents? Yes, why?"

"Do they sometimes say things like "Things were much better when I was a kid? We did not spend all day in front of a TV."

"All the time. Except now its an iPad"

"Well, imagine that but a thousand times worse. That is the Council of Vampyrs. Dullest bunch of dullards ever, and always complaining about how humans do not taste as good as they used to."

"Really?"

"Yesssss. These days 'Humans are not free range enough. Too cooped up in houses, offices and shops." Some vampyrs also think it is due to too much fast food and fizzy drinks, or all those chemicals you put in yourselves."

"Chemicals?"

"You know, shampoo, soap, deodorant, hair gel, et cetera. Taints the flavour, you know."

"Do you really have to eat-"

"Drink"

"Sorry, drink us. We really don't want to be drunk."

"Well, I am rather peckish and if I do not eat you then what should I do? Perhaps I could just drink one of you, surely your parents would not notice if only one of you was missing."

"They surely would," shouted Flora, outraged.

"Really? But there are so many humans, what is one small one between friends?" asked Sir Francis, almost pleading, looking at Henry longingly.

"In polite society, it's considered rude to eat your friends, Sir Francis" George pointedly told him, standing protectively in front of his younger brother.

"Oh, is it? Time has hardly improved things has it?"

"Why don't you try going vegan?" asked Henry, peering around from behind George's legs.

"Not you as well, it is soo trendy right now. Some of my vampyr friends have gone vegan."

"So, they've given up drinking humans and only eat plants and stuff?" asked George.

"No, they only eat vegans. However, I think that is enough, I really think I should start drinking you now. It has been very pleasant chatting with you, but my mother always told me not to play with my food."

With that he loomed towards them, seemingly growing taller, more elongated. His mouth opened and a fork like tongue licked his lips, his long yellow teeth gleaming in the fading light.

He reached out with his hands towards Henry, who had crept back around from behind George in his interest of Sir Francis. Flora was a bit further back and couldn't see what was happening.

"A bit of an aperitif first, I think."

He darted forwards and took hold of Henry's shoulders with his long thin hands, pulling him in. His eyes glowed red and seemed to mesmerise them all and George found that he could not move.

Henry was pulled into the shadow of Sir Francis, who bent down towards him, teeth closing in on Henry's pale neck.

Chapter Five

Thinking fast, Flora saw a Sharpie and a pencil in the back pocket of Henry's bag. Henry always had pens and pencils in his bag as he loved drawing: on paper, on the walls, even on himself (though mainly on himself). Usually pictures of diggers.

She grabbed them and made a cross using the Sharpy and the pencil and thrust it towards Varney. Sir Francis veered back, letting Henry go and with a snarl on his face hissed:

"Damn you, to use the cross of your Lord against me. I will return another night and drain you. Oh, hang on a minute. Did you use a marker pen for the crossbeam of the cross?"

"Erm, yes," admitted Flora.

"Well, strictly speaking that will not work as it is made of plastic. The cross needs to be all wood, or a precious metal. I am sure you understand, it is a bit of a technicality – but rules are rules. Nice try though, really good effort. Quick thinking, too."

And he lunged towards Henry, again.

As soon as Sir Francis bent down, George seemed to come round. He realised that, realistically, they couldn't fight a vampire.

"*Vampyr*" he corrected himself automatically "*rhymes with career.*"

So instead, he shouted:

"Stop!"

Sir Francis looked up, surprised.

"Cannot this wait? This little one is only a couple of mouthfuls, and then we can chat between courses – I always like to have a break."

"But I just wanted to know, why do you drink blood?"

Sir Francis stood back up, looking puzzled. He let go of Henry and looked up thoughtfully.

"Well, it keeps us alive."

"Alive?" queried Flora.

"Sorry, slip of the tongue, but you know what I mean."

"So, if you don't drink blood, do you die?" George continued.

"No, I will just get weaker and weaker, and thinner and thinner, until I will not have the strength to move. I will just lie there, conscious but unable to do anything."

"Oh, a bit like grandma, then!" said Henry cheerfully. He seemed remarkably happy despite nearly becoming a snack for a vampyr.

"But what do you need from blood?" said George. In his mind there must be a logical reason and he was determined to find it out - and to keep Sir Francis talking.

"I am not sure, I do not think anyone's ever thought about that."

"So, you are hundreds of years old, and you haven't ever thought why you can only live on blood."

"No, I suppose I never got around to it."

"Never got around to it? You're 800 years old! What have you been doing?"

"Well, some things take a bit longer to get around to doing."

"Maybe its iron" suggests Flora "there's a lot of iron in blood, from the haemo-goblin."

"Haemoglobin" corrected George, gently "but yes, maybe that's right. Perhaps you could try lots of plants with a lot of iron in them."

"I suppose it could be worth a try. Such as?"

"Well, all sorts. Hang on a minute."

Sir Francis lurched backwards, which made his left hamstring twinge a bit - he wished he had done his warmup exercises that evening. This was not working out how he had expected; he thought he would just get a quick meal and then be back home to read a good book.

Meanwhile, George got out his smartphone and quickly searched, but Sir Francis was getting impatient. And hungry. Or is it thirsty?

"Look, if it is all the same with you, I think I will just drink you tonight and think about this a bit more another time. After 800 years on the same diet, I do not know if I fancy a change yet."

Once more he lurched towards Henry, his forked tongue licking his long yellow fangs, and his eyes gleaming terribly.

Chapter Six

"How about instead of drinking people you tried eating meat?" George shouted at Sir Francis.

If he could keep Sir Francis talking, then he could hardly drink Henry at the same time. Once again Sir Francis stopped, this time mid lurch, and looked at George looking slightly pained.

"Oh please, will you stop stopping me in mid lurch – that is at least the third time. Not that I have been counting, but it is playing hell with my hamstrings. I have not had chance to limber up yet. I am sure I have pulled a muscle."

"I'm sorry, Sir Francis, but as I said again. Why don't you eat meat?"

"Eat meat? I have not eaten anything for centuries; have you seen my teeth?"

Sir Francis limped forward and opened his mouth, and they could clearly see that apart from his two (extremely long and yellow) front fangs, the rest of his mouth was empty of teeth. His breath smelt like the pits of hell - if you would happen to know what that smelt like.

"See, we do not exactly have to chew our food."

"OK, let's leave meat out then and just look at vegetables. Ah here we are. Things like spinach, chard, kidney beans...."

"What, you can get beans made from kidneys? Sounds horrible! They must taste like wee." said Sir Francis, clearly alarmed.

"No, they just look like kidneys."

"Ah."

"Dried fruit, nuts, tofu."

"Tofu?"

"Yes, it's a meat substitute made of bean curd."

"Sounds revolting."

"Wait until you hear about Quorn then. It's made from fungus."

"Fungus? Like mushrooms?"

"Yep, but I wouldn't worry. That's not good for iron."

"So, you have seen my teeth. How do you propose that I eat any of this?" enquired Sir Francis.

"Maybe we could borrow grandpa's teeth." asked Henry.

"No, we can't, Henry. It's bad enough he keeps losing them." replied George.

"I found them in my toy box last time he stayed over." said Flora, making a sick gesture with her fingers.

"Maybe we could liquidise it all. You both remember when Mum went on that daft smoothie diet?"

Flora and Henry nodded.

"She got that really expensive food liquidiser. I'm sure it's in the back of the cupboard gathering dust. Sir Francis, how about we make a deal?"

"Well, possibly. What do you suggest my boy?"

"Well, you don't drink us tonight, and we will come back tomorrow with some food high in iron, liquidised-"

"Liquidised. How do you mean?"

"Well, we have a machine that whizzes all the food together and turns it into a liquid."

"Hmm, clever. So, I do not drink you tonight, and you bring me food to drink tomorrow? And then can I drink you after that?"

"No! You don't drink us then! The idea is to find something you can live on that doesn't involve murder."

"Oh, that does not sound so good to me. And it is not really murder."

"Not murder? What would you call it?"

"Well, not murder. That is what one human does to another. And, as you can see, I am no longer human. You do not murder a chicken when you eat it."

"Well, OK, but you won't kill us."

"I suppose not" Sir Francis replied, unhappily.

"Well, we had better be on our way. So, we'll come round tomorrow night after school?"

"Yesssss, I will be here, waiting," Sir Francis replied, rather menacingly.

"Well, we had best be going, otherwise Mother will wonder what's happened to us."

"Nothing unfortunately." said Sir Francis sullenly.

The three kids glared at him.

"Sorry." he said, meekly.

The three turned to leave and walk the short distance to their house. They started off, and then George stopped, turned, and looked straight at Sir Francis.

"Oh, and Sir Francis, no drinking anyone else"

"Oh blast" grumbled Varney "Yesssss of course. No drinking"

He sounded seriously deflated. Like a flattened whoopee cushion.

"Cross your heart."

"Cross? Cross my heart? How very dare you."

"Oh, sorry. Would that hurt?"

"Yesssss. A lot."

"OK just promise then."

"I promise." the gloomy vampire, sorry, vampyr (rhymes with appear) replied.

"See you tomorrow. Oh, by the way, I'm George, and this is Flora and Henry."

"Enchanted to make your acquaintance." he raised his arms up, seemingly welcoming them.

"What?" asked Henry.

"He means nice to meet you" explained George, but something was bothering him.

"So, you've lived in that house a long time?"

"Yesssss, a very long time"

"So how come we haven't seen you before, or there hasn't been reports of people being drunk."

"Like dad when he used to come back from the pub?" asked Henry, cheerfully.

"No Henry, I meant drunk as being... drunk. You know – by a vampyr."

"Ah."

"Anyway, Sir Francis, how come we've only just met you? We've lived here all our lives, and no one ever mentioned a vampyr."

"Oh well that's good. I have not been around much recently as I have had a bit of a lie in."

"So, you had a sleep in, like dad did at weekends."

"Maybe. Not sure it is exactly the same."

"So, when did you go to bed?"

"1992 I think."

"Oh" exclaimed George "that would explain it. Anyway, we must be going. Bye."

And with that, they set off back home.

Chapter Seven

Varney watched them walk up the street. He was puzzled. He was starving, but he really didn't regret not drinking the children. They were the first people he had spoken to in years. No, decades. Maybe it would be nice to have friends, he decided, and George could be right. It could be rude to drink your friends.

"Friends," he thought "What a strange term" but the more he thought about it, the more he seemed to like the idea.

He remained there in the shadows, thinking about trying to find someone else for a quick snack, but then he decided it only seemed right to keep his promise. He really did not want to be thought of as a liar, or a cad or a bounder - like those horrid wraiths. Horrible creatures. Always lying and trying to steal other people's precious things.

Yes, he thought, he would just stay hungry tonight. But tomorrow night? He would see.

Little did he know that whilst he was thinking all of this, somewhere from a darkened attic window a few houses down, a pair of high-powered binoculars were trained on him.

"Is that definitely him?" said Mr. Sticks, to the man, or whatever, holding the binoculars.

"**YES, WITHOUT A DOUBT.**" replied Mr. Stones.

"Finally. Then we can begin."

Chapter Eight

The kids arrived back at 99 Shackledown Road a few minutes later and burst into the kitchen. Mrs. Bannerworth was busy in the kitchen, creating some sort of experimental pasta dish for their tea.

Experimental was code for the fact that she hadn't been to the shops and so was just making something out of whatever was in the fridge. Sometimes she produced a triumph of a dish that everyone loved, but more often they ended up at the disastrous end of the culinary spectrum.

As she cooked, she took an occasional sip out of a tall, thin stemmed glass, which had a straw-yellow fizzy liquid in it. Mrs. Bannerworth liked things with bubbles - baths and drinks especially.

She hummed to herself as she cooked, as the radio was on in the background, Radio 1 of course. Mrs. Bannerworth still clung to the idea that listening to Radio 1 helped your kids think you were cool. Frankly, the kids couldn't care less as they could not see the point of the radio when there was Spotify. Why did you want to listen to old people talking in between your music?

"Where have you three been? I expected you back a good hour ago."

"We're sorry, Mother, we missed the bus and had to walk," explained George.

"Oh, not again. Whose fault was it this time?" she asked, staring suspiciously at Flora and Henry.

"No, it was my fault," said George, gallantly - he didn't like getting the little ones into trouble.

"Mmhmm, sure," said Mum, suspiciously, but she decided not to push the matter any more.

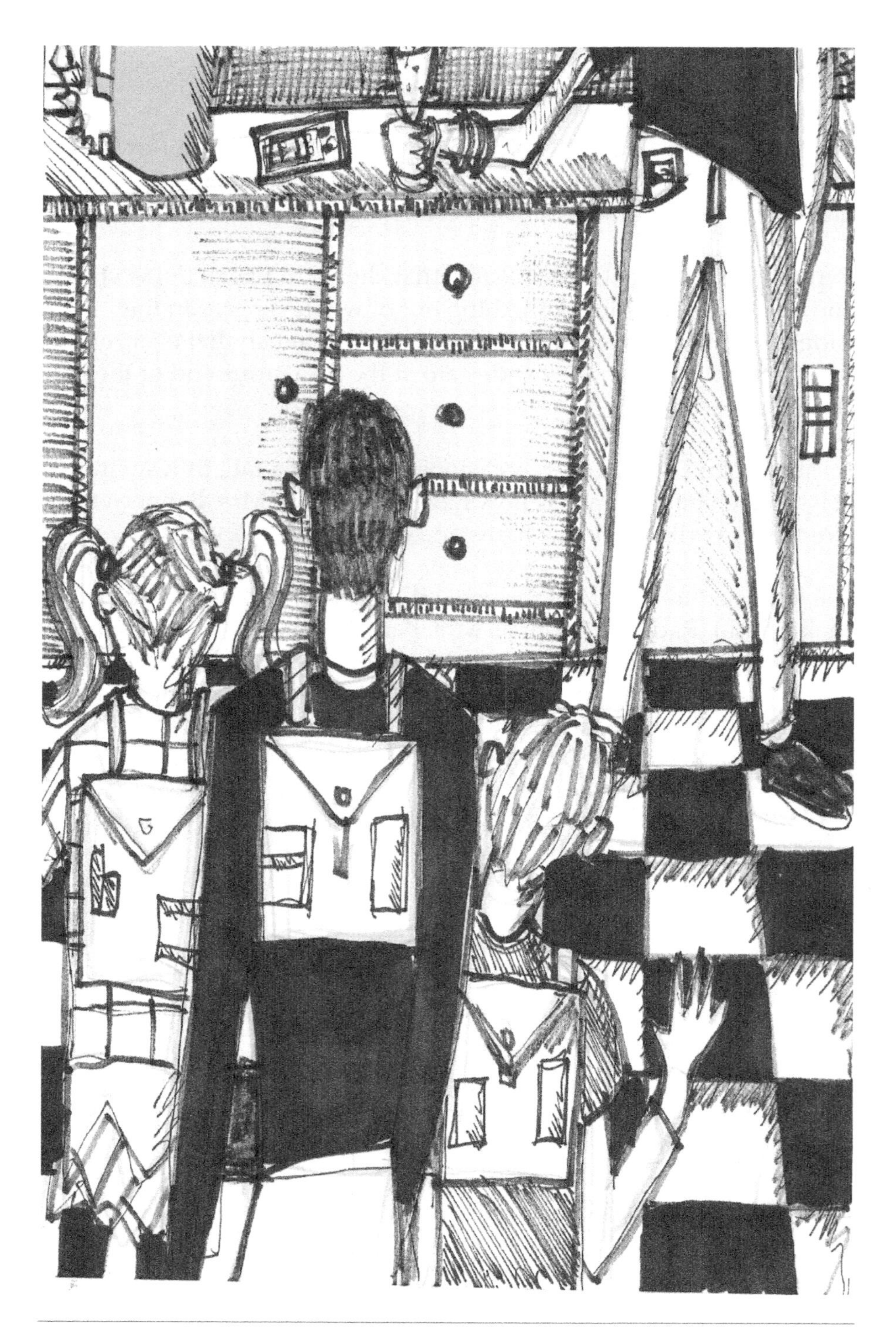

"Mama," asked Henry "Do you know the house at the end of the road?"

George tried to shush Henry, but to no avail.

"The big, dark one?"

"Yes. Do you know who lives there?"

"No, I don't think anyone does," Mum replied.

"Yes, there is" shouted Flora and Henry in unison.

"He's called Sir Francis Varney!" said Flora.

"And he's over 80 years old" continued Henry.

"800, Henry."

"Sorry, 800 years old."

"And he's a vampire."

"Vampyr, rhymes with cheer," corrected George, unable to help himself, and realising now that there was no chance of keeping this quiet.

"He's a bit odd looking, Mummy. He's got a big head, and two big, pointed teeth."

"And red eyes, and pointy ears," supplied Henry.

"He was a bit scary at first, as he wanted to drink us," Flora continued, a bit irritated by Henry chipping in all the time. It was her story, after all. The others just happened to be there.

"He wanted to have a drink with you," asked Mummy "I've told you about not accepting anything from strangers."

"No drink us, Mama!" shouted Henry, jumping up and down with excitement.

"Drink our blood, Mummy, as he's a vampire."

"Vampyr, rhymes with fear," George tried again. He stood at the back, letting the other two talk away.

"Now, kids, there's no such thing as a vampire," Mother / Mummy / Mama replied.

"ITS VAMPYR, RHYMES WITH SPEAR," shouted all three in unison, even George couldn't resist getting involved.

"OK," said Mum, shaking her head "vampYR," she replied.

"What's going on in here? What's everyone excited about," asked a deep male voice from behind the girls.

"Mr. Marchdale, the kids were just telling me how they met a real live vampire…"

All three kids were about to shout out.

"Sorry, vampyr. Rhymes with shear," she corrected.

"A vampyr, you say, Mrs. Bannerworth? Well, who'd have thought it?"

Chapter Nine

Mr. Marchdale is a lodger who lives in the garage while he is working in the town. Though perhaps garage is an underhand word as it is not a grimy old building full or rusty tools and greasy car parts, it had been quite nicely converted into a separate bedroom and bathroom a few years ago. It's not like he was sleeping on a dog bed in a drafty old room.

He lives there about 3 weeks every month, then he would disappear for a week or so, back home. No one knew where "back home" was, and no one really thought to ask. He worked in town doing something or other, and sometimes kept odd hours.

He was of medium height, with broad shoulders, thin spindly legs, and thick brown hair, cut in a very old fashion – centre parted and quite long, with huge bushy sideburns. His eyes were an almost hazel colour, and hidden beneath thick shaggy eyebrows. He normally wore a tweed three-piece suit, which had seen better days, and almost always a deerstalker hat – even in the house. He spoke with a vaguely northern accent, but it was hard to pin down which part of the north - or even the north of which country.

The kids all loved him like they would an older, slightly odd uncle. He helped around the house, helped look after the kids, helped them with their homework, and liked to entertain them with wild and outlandish stories.

He had a strange relationship with their Mother. They were very formal with each other and would only call each other by their surnames. Typically:

"Hello, Mr. Marchdale."

"Good morning to you, Mrs. Bannerworth."

The kids didn't even know his first name and called him Mr. March for short, which he didn't seem not to mind too much.

"Yes, a vampyr, apparently, Mr. Marchdale. He lives in Ratford House, the big old pile at the end of the road."

"Ahh, yes, the spooky house" replied Mr. March, raising his hands above his head, pretending to be a ghost dancing around and pretending to lunge at the kids. The children laughed their heads off at his antics.

"Mr. Marchdale, be serious."

"My apologies, Mrs. Bannerworth. Please continue."

"But I've never seen anyone anywhere near that house," Mrs. Bannerworth continued.

"Hmm, me neither. Odd. Very odd," Mr. March agreed.

"Yes, well he explained that" continued George, deciding it was about time he said his piece "He's lived there for a long time, but has been having a lie in – apparently he went to bed in 1992."

"1992?"

"Yes, it was an exceptionally long lie in, but then he is 800 years old. Or so he says."

"So, you say he wanted to eat you?" queried Mr. March.

"No, drink" snapped Flora "he's only got two teeth, so he doesn't eat anything."

"Righto, drink. Your blood I suppose."

"Yes" Said George "but he didn't seem that determined, he seemed to be happy having a chat. He seemed very lonely."

"And he agreed not to drink us!" shouted Henry.

"Because we said we could find him something else to drink," finished Flora.

"So Mother, can we borrow that food blender you have, the one you never use any more? We've got an experiment to try" enquired George.

Mother sighed. She was well used to George's experiments, but she also knew that whatever he did would be safe and well thought through.

"Yes, I suppose so. Just don't make a mess."

"Great thanks Mother," said George, thankfully "Right, Flora, Henry lets go in the lounge and plan what we need to do tomorrow."

"I'll shout you when tea is ready."

"Thanks mommy."

"Well," mommy said to Mr. March "what do you make of that? Such imaginations! They've met a vampire."

"Vampyr, rhymes with…"

"Oh, not you as well, Mr. Marchdale. Vampyr then. But the poor man is probably just a bit odd. If he even exists."

Mr. March said nothing but looked deep in thought.

After dinner, or tea, or whatever you want to call it, the kids raided the kitchen. The found spinach, kale, nuts and dried fruit, and vegetables that they had found out were high in iron. Then they spend a couple of hours with the blender, whizzing things together and putting them in plastic cups, before Mum one by one sent them to bed.

Chapter Ten

The next day dragged at school, all the kids could think about was going back around to Ratford House and trying to 'fix' Sir Francis' drink problem. As soon as the bell went that afternoon, they all ran to the bus stop, and were first on the bus.

The bus driver, Jack Pringle, cheerfully welcomed the Bannerworth children.

"Hullo, George, Flora and Henry! You are early tonight, you're normally running up to the bus as I am about to drive off."

"Hello, Jack Pringle. Not today. We have an experiment to do," explained George, cryptically.

"Yes, with a vam- ouch!" Henry didn't get any further as Flora kicked him in the shin, not too hard but hard enough.

"Oh, an experiment you say? What's it about?" Jack continued, he was very friendly and loved to talk.

"I'm sorry, its top secret," said George.

"Eyes only," said Flora, not really knowing what the meant, but she was sure she had heard it on the TV after the spy said Top Secret.

"Oh, OK," said Jack, looking a bit crestfallen.

Then, stopping any more questions, more kids arrived and the three of them made their way down the bus to some seats.

The half hour journey seemed to last forever, but then they were at the end of their road. They ran down the road to their door and burst through it. In a flurry of throwing bags down, grabbing other bags, within a few minutes they had all their kit.

They set off down the road, back to the far end of the street by the snickett. There, Ratford House seemed to loom towards them, dark and menacing in the late afternoon gloom. They were a bit early and were worried if Sir Francis was even out of bed yet - or out of his coffin. George made a mental note to ask Sir Francis about this when he got chance.

"Do you think he's still here?" asked Flora.

"Hmm, maybe we should go and knock on his door," said George, thinking aloud.

"Well, I suppose we could," said Flora nervously. Henry looked a little scared.

"It's just a house," George said placating them both.

They opened the crooked gate and walked up the crooked path to the crooked front door. It was green but the paint was peeling off in places. George reached for the handle and pushed the green door. Immediately behind it in the hallway was an old piano, but no one was playing it.

"Sir Francis are you in there?" shouted George through the open door, his voice echoing around the house.

No answer.

"Frank?" called Henry.

Again, no answer.

"Well, we are here, so we don't want to turn back, do we?" asked George of the others.

Both Flora and Henry shook their heads, bravely.

As one, they stepped in through the door and a few steps into the house. As soon as they did, they heard a bang behind them. They all spun and noticed the door has slammed shut. They looked at each other, near panic on their faces.

They were in a large open hallway. The piano was on the wall, close to the door, but it was covered in dust and cobwebs. Two flights of stairs went up from the hallway, on each side of the room, up to a long landing above. There were several wall lights, but they were unlit, and the only light came from a large chandelier in the centre of the tall ceiling. It was lit with 13 candles that spluttered away, casting a dim amber light. The floor was bare boards, some broken, cockroaches and other insects scurrying across them. From the wainscoting, they could hear the scratching of tiny claws, mice or rats that have obviously made their homes in the walls.

They were about to run for the door and try to wrench it open when they heard a deep booming voice.

Chapter Eleven

"Ah, George, Flora and Henry. So good of you to visit."

Sir Francis appeared from a door across the hallway. He almost seemed to float across the floor towards them.

"My apologies for the door. I had the back door open as I was hanging the washing up in the back garden - must have been a breeze. Nothing supernatural, I can assure you."

Henry looked crestfallen that the door did not close due to magic or some supernatural entity.

"Washing? Vampyrs do washing?" asked Flora in astonishment.

"Well, of course. You know how easily black shows the dirt and mud. Just because I do not have any mirrors does not mean that I do not try to look my best."

"No mirrors?" said Henry, amazed.

"Well, yesssss, you do know that vampyrs cast no reflection?"

"They can't be seen in mirrors, and they cast no shadows." explained George to Henry.

"Ah, ok"

"But it's not quite dark yet and you were outside. I thought daylight killed you?"

"Well first, it is very shaded in the back garden so no direct sun. But no, I can still walk around in daylight, I prefer not to" replied Sir Francis, haughtily.

"Why?"

"Well, if you must know, three reasons really. It gives me terrible dermatitis of the scalp and a bit of a headache."

"And what's the third reason?"

"I do not really want to say..."

"Oh, go on Frank."

"Oh, all right. People tend to stare."

"Can I just ask, Sir Francis? You look a bit different today. Yesterday you were very pale, but today your skin seems even more blue."

"Oh, that. Well, it is a bit embarrassing. The thirstier I am, the bluer I become."

"Do all vampyrs do that?" asked Flora.

"It is different for us all, each of us seems to turn out slightly differently with our own peculiarities. It is all a bit of a lottery, look at Vlad - tall dark and handsome."

"You are tall, and dress in black" said Flora gently,

"And a bit gruesome" commented Henry, happily.

Sir Francis looked a bit hurt by that.

George had been thinking, and carried on,

"So, it's the lack of blood that's turning you blue. That's what humans do, when their blood turns blue as it's not oxygenated. Therefore, you may be blue due to the lack of oxygen"

"But I do not need oxygen to breathe, as I do not breathe." said Sir Francis.

"But that makes no sense!" said George, frustrated that his impeccable logic was incorrect.

"I know, but that is how it is with us supernaturals - not everything makes sense. Sometimes it seems that someone is just making it all up."

Sir Francis looked a bit sad for a moment, but then he picked himself up.

"Anyway, welcome to Ratford House, my humble home, as it has been, on and off, for centuries," said Sir Francis, bowing deeply, and theatrically "please, shall we make our way to the parlour?"

Sir Francis pointed at a door with one exceedingly long arm with extremely long fingers.

The children looked at each other and shrugged.

Sir Francis glided across the floor in front of them, his feet seemingly a few inches above the ground. He gestured, and the door swung inwards.

"Oh, that was cool!" said Henry.

Sir Francis smiled, not the nicest of smiles as it just made his long fangs more pronounced.

"Come, come inside. Once you are a guest in my house, then you will not be harmed."

"Is that some sort of vampyric law or rule? A bit like we have to invite vampyrs in?" asked George.

"No, it is simply good manners. What would I be as a host if all my guests were always drunk?" replied Sir Francis.

Chapter Twelve

It was a comfortable living room/parlour, or it would have been 100 years ago. Plush chairs and settees surrounded a low coffee table though the fabric of the seats was torn, and the stuffing was peeking through. On the wall were dusty old portraits of men, women, and children all dressed in old fashioned clothes along with a couple of tattered old tapestries.

On one wall was a set of bookcases from floor to ceiling - they were crammed with books, magazines and even what looked like scrolls. The books were all leather or fabric bound, and the golden embossed writing had faded on their spines. On another wall was a tall dresser, on top was a decanter and several lead crystal glasses arranged on a tarnished silver tray.

Next to the dresser was a tall wine rack, filled with dusty old bottles of green and brown. George walked over, wiping his finger along one of the shelves of the bookcase, leaving a trail in the dust. He inspected his finger and seeing the dust he huffed to himself, he loved books and disliked seeing them in such a state of neglect.

He walked over to the dresser and pulled a brown bottle from the wine rack, rubbing the thin film of dust from the label.

"What's this bottle? The label says Napoleon? Oh, so it's Napoleon Brandy. My dad used to drink that."

Varney floated over and seemed to hover next to him, looking down enquiringly.

"Brandy? No, that IS Napoleon," he answered.

"What?"

"Napoleon."

"The ruler of France?"

Varney nods, "That's the very fellow - not very tall and a bit pompous," and took the bottle off George and carefully places it back on the shelf.

"It is an incredibly old vintage, but I am not supposed to open it for another 100 years. It was a present from a lady."

"Really, what was she called?"

"Josephine, I seem to recall. She gave it to me one night when she had been stood up."

Flora and Henry were looking around and found an old dog bed behind one of the sofas.

"Do you have a dog?" Flora asked.

"A dog, no. Curs and mutts they are... Sorry, got a bit carried away. No, I used to have a werewolf and that was his bed. Well, some of the time, when he was in wolf form. He seems to have wandered off."

"But I thought vampyrs and werewolves were natural enemies. They are in the films, like the ones with the twinkly vampyrs."

"Twinkly vampyrs? I know not what you talk of. Films, pah, rubbish. First of all, vampyrs and werewolves are supernatural, not natural.

Secondly, we vampyrs quite like werewolves. You know how you humans keep dogs as pets? Well, some vampyrs keep werewolves. If you can get over the howling and the shedding, of skin and fur, they are quite good company. Not good to talk to of course, as they are about as bright as your average Labrador, but nice to have around as they trot around after you and are always pleased to see you when you get back after a long night of drinking.

However, they do make a mess of the garden and the skirting boards." Sir Francis lamented.

"What was he called?" asked Henry.

"He who?"

"The werewolf?"

"So, you are assuming it was a male? You do get female werewolves as well."

"Oh sorry, so was its girl?" said Henry looking a bit unsure.

"No, it was a male, he was called Maximus. I should have gotten someone to wolf-sit for him when I had my lie in, oh well."

"So, was he called Max for short?" asked Flora.

"No, Maximus. Why are all you humans so keen to shorten everything. I suppose that is the advantage of living forever, you do not need to shorten words all the time."

"But you asked us to call you Frank."

"Well, yesssss, but to be honest, Sir Francis does sound a bit pompous. I thought it would make you more relaxed before I drank you if you knew me as Frank" said Sir Francis.

"Ah, yes Sir Fr- sorry- Frank. We had some ideas about your drinking problem" said George, seizing the opportunity to talk about their experiments.

"Drinking problem? I am not sure I like that tone."

"No, not that. The problem that you have to drink blood."

"Ah, yes."

"Well, try this." George rummaged in the backpack he was carrying. He pulled out a plastic cup with a lid and a straw. Sloshing around in it was a thick, green liquid and passed it to Sir Francis, sorry, to Frank.

The vampyr took it in his long spindly fingers and pulled the lid off and sniffed it.

"Well, it does not smell too revolting. It seems to have a similar type of smell to blood, quite an acrid smell. Well, here she goes."

He opened his mouth, it expanded like a snake unhinging his jaw, until his face was almost twice as long as it normally was. Then he put the cup to his mouth and took a long swig of the green viscous liquid.

The children watched eagerly, and then Sir Francis stopped drinking, and spat a mouthful off the slimy concoction all over the worn rug.

"IT ISS COLD!" he shouted, looking disgusted.

"Well, it has been in the fridge," countered George.

"One of the first things you notice about blood, George my boy, is that it is not served cold. It is served at a human temperature, exactly 37 degrees Celsius!"

"Oh, never thought of that," admitted George.

Chapter Thirteen

"Have you got a microwave?" asked Flora.

"Now why would I have a microwave? It is hardly like I keep any food in the house," replied Sir Francis.

"Flora," said George, thinking on his feet "run back home and use the one in our house. You've got your key?"

"Yep, will do," and with that Flora grabbed the plastic cup out of Sir Francis' extremely long fingers, and ran out of the room to the front door.

For a few moments, George, Henry, and Sir Francis just sat there in an awkward silence, looking around the room and trying to avoid eye contact. Then George decided to break the silence. He still had 1001 questions for Sir Francis about life as a vampyr.

"Sooo," he started. Sir Francis looked up at him, interested "Is it true that vampyrs hate garlic?"

"No, I quite like it - the smell of it anyway."

"But all the books say that garlic wards off vampyrs?"

"Well, it does, sort of, it makes your blood taste funny. And it gives me terrible wind."

"But it doesn't harm you."

"No, you have been reading too many books."

George loved books and would get through them at about the same rate most people got through meals – three a day. George was about to carry on questioning Sir Francis when the door flew open, and

Flora dashed into the parlour. She was holding the cup and shoved it in Sir Francis long, pale face.

"There, I measured it, it was exactly 37 degrees when it came out of the microwave."

"Very well, I suppose I should try it then," said Sir Francis.

He took the cup, flipped off the top, and took his first long gulp of the thick, green liquid inside.

Sir Francis finished the cup down to the dregs, then licking his lips with an unfeasibly long tongue.

Immediately something strange started to happen, his skin colour started changing. Originally, he had a blue tinge to his skin, but now a green hue started to creep up his face climbing up from his long pale neck.

The colour slowly crept up his face, and fullness started to fill his thin cheeks. Suddenly, Sir Francis didn't look quite so cadaverous. His eyes changes from a bright red to a vivid green, like a pair of emeralds gleaming out. He looked at his hands, and his fingers started to become a little thicker and the long fingernails were no longer chipped and broken.

"Sir Francis," shouted Flora "what's happening to your head?"

Sir Francis could feel a strange sensation in his bald scalp. Then it felt like his head was getting taller or longer.

"Your hair!" shouted George.

"What hair?"

He put his hands up to his large head and it felt fluffy, and this fluff he could feel was getting thicker and denser - more hair like.

For the first time in 650 years, he had hair.

"Well, that is odd." exclaimed Sir Francis "What does it look like? My hair?"

"Well, it's mainly black."

"Mainly black?"

"Well, it's sort of black but with green in it."

"I have green hair?!" Sir Francis exclaimed, amazed.

"Well, only a little bit green. How do you feel?"

"Pretty good. In fact, I feel fantastic," replied Sir Francis.

"Fangtastic," joked Henry, giggling, doing a pretty good impersonation of Sir Francis.

Sir Francis looked around at Henry and smiled. Then he reached down and took hold of the leg of the sofa Henry was sitting on. He picked the couch, and Henry, up by the one leg and held it above his head.

"Whoa" cried Henry, grinning with joy as he found himself nearing the cracked ceiling whilst holding onto the sofa.

Sir Francis put the couch down gently.

"Again! Again!" Henry shouted, delighted.

"Perhaps later," he grinned.

"How did it taste Sir Francis?"

"Not bad," he admitted, "Makes a change from blood. Blood becomes pretty boring after 800 years. All the O positive is so dull and bland, no body to it"

"What's the tastiest blood type?" Queried George.

"Oh, AB negative of course. It has a bit of spice to it, though there is not much of it around."

"So can you do everything that you normally could as a vampyr?" George wondered.

"Good question, I suppose I can try. What shall I do first?" he asked.

"Turn into a bat!" suggested Flora.

"Good idea, I have not had a good fly around for a while."

He concentrated, and then there was a 'puff' sound and a cloud of green smoke. Hanging in the air, where Sir Francis had just been, was a small green animal. It had brown eyes, green fur, and a long bushy green tail. In between its four legs was webbed skin, and the creature flapped its limbs wildly as it tried to stay airborne.

Then it started to plummet towards the ground.

Chapter Fourteen

"A squirrel! You've turned into a flying squirre,l" shouted Flora, delighted with the phenomena before her.

She loved squirrels, especially red ones, and had always wanted one for a pet. Already she had started to think about if she could make a cage for Sir Francis and keep him as a pet. A green squirrel would be even better than a red one, and all her friends would be jealous.

But then she thought Sir Francis might get a bit annoyed and turn back and ruin the cage or end up trapped inside with his arms and legs stuck through the bars.

Sir Francis the flying green squirrel meanwhile sort of managed to stop his plummet and fly around the room. As flying squirrels do not really fly but glide, he had to work awfully hard to keep afloat. It was hardly a smooth flight, as he kept bumping up against the roof and crashed more than once into the furniture.

Then he started to drop to the floor, and there was another 'puff' and a cloud of smoke, Sir Francis was himself again. He seemed exhausted and was breathing heavily, which seemed a bit odd to the kids, as they knew he didn't need to breathe.

"That was... Interesting" said Sir Francis "not quite what I expected."

"Do it again, do it again!" shouted Henry, jumping up and down in excitement.

"I think not." said Sir Francis.

"Then turn into mist. Or into a wolf. Or into a load of rats. Or into a rabbit," demanded Henry.

"A rabbit? Vampyrs do not turn into rabbits, young man," replied Sir Francis indignantly, "No, and I think that is quite enough for now."

"So, do you feel like you need to go out for a drink now?" asked George.

"No, I feel quite full thank you. Apart from surprising side effects, of course, but perhaps I can get used to that."

"Excellent," said George.

"Super," said Flora.

"Great," said Henry.

"How often do you need to feed?" George asked "so we know when to bring you the next one."

"Tomorrow would be grand," said Sir Francis.

"OK, well we had better go, Mother said that we had to be back for tea at six. Goodbye Sir Francis, see you tomorrow!"

"Yesssss thank you all and farewell. I feel so much better and do not have to worry about going out to eat, sorry, drink, tonight."

George beckoned to Flora and Henry, who grumpily got up off the sofa. They waved goodbye and walked across to the doorway.

Sir Francis sat down on the sofa, looking pretty happy.

All in all, he thought, that had gone rather well. He was pleased as he really liked George, Flora and Henry and it would have been a real shame to have drunk them.

Unknown to Sir Francis, outside at the window, in the chilly night air, hidden in the dark were two faces. They peered through the dusty panes of glass into the parlour, unseen.

One face was long and thin, with a beak-like nose, thin lips and pallid cheeks. The eyes were small, brown, pig-like and darted from side to side. He had pale, limp hair that was pasted to his forehead. His face was one of the most untrustworthy faces you could possibly imagine.

The other face was almost square, with a big square nose, big square ears and even, it seemed, big square eyes. The eyes were cold, grey, and emotionless - as was the skin, somehow. The thick grey hair on his head stuck up in spikes, making him look like an aging villain from an old action film.

"Well, they've finally gone, Mr. Stones," spoke the smaller man from his thin lips. His voice was quick, high pitched and his manner animated.

"**SO IT APPEARS, MR. STICKS,**" rumbled the larger man, in a flat emotionless tone, face hardly seeming to move as he spoke. "**DO WE BEGIN?**"

"Not yet. Surveillance first, then we act. That's what our employee asked for. We don't want to do anything precipitous."

"**SO BE IT**" growled Mr. Stones, a bit frustrated - he wanted to act.

But they would wait.

Chapter Fifteen

The next few days fell into a routine. On school days, the kids were now never late for the bus. In fact, they were always first on. As soon as they got home, they would drop of their bags, warm up a cup of the green sludge, and run around to Ratford House as soon as dusk fell.

They opened the already open crooked gate, sprint up the crooked path and in through the crooked door. Sir Francis would normally be waiting, hungry (or is it thirsty?) for the green blood replacement - which Henry had decided to call glood, rhymes with mud. Or blood.

Sir Francis would gulp down the glood like a man who had been stranded in a desert for a week. Each time Sir Francis drank some glood, his hair grew a bit more, his skin turned a bit greener, and his eyes glowed bright like emeralds.

The glood continued to have strange side effects: when Henry and Flora persuaded Sir Francis to turn into mist, instead he ended up as a pile of green goop on the floor - something a bit like a cross between slime and jelly.

However, Sir Francis found that he could still move and slip under the cracks in windows and doors, he quite liked the slippery sensation as he slid along surfaces. He had never really liked turning into mist, it was all a bit discombobulating. It felt as if he was all spread out into various different bodies, so when he turned back to his vampyric form, he literally had to pull himself together.

However, one thing about turning into goop was that he left a thin trail, like a very large slug (or lots of small slugs side by side - but slugs aren't very good at synchronised sliding). It was a sticky, slimy trail. It amused Sir Francis no end that if he went back to his old ways and slipped under the door to drink someone, then the occupants of the house would be more than puzzled as to why there seemed to be an infestation of slugs. However, that was unlikely, as if he drunk blood again, he would likely lose this ability.

What happened when he tried to turn into a mischief of rats? We won't go into it. It did not end well.

However, Sir Francis felt unnaturally (naturally) good and healthy - he walked, or glided, with a spring in his step. The kids enjoyed his company immensely, as he had lots of tall stories, and most of them were even partly true. Sir Francis also enjoyed their company and realised that over the last few centuries he had been alone.

If it were a weekend, the kids would wait, staring at the clock and glancing out of the window, waiting for the sun to start to dip below the horizon. It seemed to take forever, even though it was winter in England, and everyone knows the sun is only seen about 4 hours a day in the winter in England. But to the kids, those few hours seemed like 4 days. As soon as the sun started to fall, they would dash around to Ratford House as quick as they could.

Mrs. Bannerworth and Mr. March seemed to take it all in their stride. Mrs. Bannerworth did not for one minute believe that they were going to see a vampire. Sorry - Vampyr, rhymes with leer. She just assumed that they were playing in the gardens of the spooky house, but she trusted George, and so knew they were safe.

What Mr. March thought was hard to tell.

However, as the kids went back and forth from Ratford House, they mostly failed to notice two figures who were often lurking. One was small and thin, with greasy pale hair, the other tall and almost square, seemingly carved from granite.

Occasionally, George would see a thin shadow from around a corner, or a pair of grey eyes staring at them, but he thought nothing of it. He did not realise they were being watched.

He would be alarmed to find out that a house on Shackledown Road, somewhere between No.99 and Ratford House, on the opposite side of the road, was a room in the attic. From the window were pointed cameras, aimed at their house and Sir Francis' home - videos filmed 24 hours a day.

In this room, every inch of the wall was covered in photographs of the kids with Sir Francis (well, probably with Sir Francis as he did not appear in photos). There were transcripts of conversations, notes with timings, descriptions, and every coming and going between Ratford House and No.99, with maps of each house.

Around a table at the end of the room sat Mr. Sticks and Mr. Stones. In the centre of the table was a phone, an old phone with a dial and a curly wire. The phone rang - Mr. Sticks picked it up and listened. He did not need to ask who it was, or say who he was, as only one person called this phone.

He listened attentively. He nodded his head every now and then (not that the person at the other end of the phone would see him). He put the phone down after about 2 minutes, having not ever said a word.

"Miss Words tells me that our employer wants us to facilitate the extraction tomorrow" said Mr. Sticks.

"**TOMORROW?**" repeated Mr. Stones.

"Yes. Tomorrow."

"**FINALLY,**" said Mr. Stones. "**DURING THE DAY?**"

"Yes, during the day."

Chapter Sixteen

Bright and early on Monday morning, the kids left as usual for school. George first, as always, followed by Flora and then running after them was Henry. As usual, Henry had only just managed to grab his coat and school bag before running out of the house.

Watching them were Sticks and Stones. Mr. Sticks followed them at a distance to make sure they got on the bus; Mr. Stones watched the house. Mrs. Bannerworth and Mr. March had never tried to visit Ratford House, but Mr. Stones has watched humans for a long time and knew how unpredictable they could be. He watched as Mrs. Bannerworth rushed out of the house, running to get the bus to work, and then half an hour later Mr. March finally left and headed into town, strolling and whistling as he went. Mr. March never went anywhere in a hurry, as he felt there was nowhere worth hurrying towards.

Mr. Sticks returned from the bus stop and met up with Mr. Stones.

"Mrs. Bannerworth?" he asked.

"**GONE. WORK,**" replied Mr. Stones.

"Mr. Marchdale?"

"**GONE. WHEREVER.**"

Their surveillance had still not uncovered what Mr. Marchdale did each day, but he was not the main concern. He was out of the way, that was all that was important.

"Excellent, we are good to go."

"**ABOUT TIME.**"

Mr. Stones walked off and went back to the house they were 'borrowing'. They were not really renting as the owners didn't even know they were there, but they hadn't stolen it as they would soon leave when their assignment was over. So borrowed seemed appropriate.

He went inside and a few moments later came out carrying a couple of large black duffel bags. From the way they moved they were obviously heavy, but Mr. Stones carried them both one handed, with as much effort as it takes a toddler to carry a soft toy.

They both walked up and opened the already open crooked gate and started up the crooked path.

There is something odd about houses: the longer the same person lives in a house, the more the house soaks up part of the essence of the resident. It's hardly noticeable in human houses, as people are always moving. From flat to terrace house, then a nice semi in the suburbs, then a lovely house in the country. A forever house that never was forever. People never seemed to stay still these days.

Sir Francis, however, has lived in the same house for over 500 years. Over that time, the house had become almost sentient- almost awake. Like it was a part of Sir Francis. Over that time, the house had sometimes oozed menace to deter people from visiting, it had sometimes shrouded itself in darkness, so everyone forgot it was there. Otherwise, by now property developers would have torn it down, and built flats on the land.

Mr. Sticks and Mr. Stones should have remembered this, but they were about to be reminded of it.

They walked up the crooked path and stood in front of the crooked door. Mr. Stones pointed at the door, Mr. Sticks shook his head and pointed to go around the side. They walked around the left side of the house and found a window. It was a large, old fashioned sash window - Mr. Stones pointed, and Mr. Sticks nodded.

Mr. Stones put down the bags and unzipped one, he put his arm in, all the way up to the shoulder and rummaged around. That was odd in itself, as the bag was only as deep as his elbow. Eventually he grunted in triumph and pulled out a large crowbar that was at least 3 foot long. Which was also odd, as the bag was only 2 foot long. He placed the crowbar on the window ledge and slipped the thin end under the window frame and pushed down. Dried paint and wood swollen with age resisted, as Mr. Stones heaved on the bar. He tried once, then again, and on the third time it, as usual, worked like a charm. The frame shifted up with a screech, only a few inches but that was enough.

Mr. Stones dropped the bar bag into the unzipped bag, it seemed to fall inside the bag for a few seconds until it finally came to rest with a 'thunk'. Then he put his shovel-like hands under the window frame and heaved up. The window shrieked as it was wrenched open, unable to resist Mr. Stone's prestigious strength.

Mr. Sticks smiled thinly, reached up and grabbed the window sill to haul himself up. As his fingers took hold of the sill, Ratford House acted. The heavy sash window slammed back down, straight onto both of Mr. Stick's hands. His fingers snapped like dried twigs, and he let out a high-pitched screech.

He pulled his hands back and saw that all his fingers had snapped off, the twig-like fingers were crushed under the window and still wriggled with minds of their own. He looked down at the stumps of what was left of his thin fingers and concentrated. Slowly, tendrils started to grow from the stumps, intertwining until they formed new fingers. He flexed his new digits, getting used to the feel of them and grimaced slightly as they were still stiff.

Mr. Stones just stared at Mr. Sticks with his cold grey eyes.

"Hm, interesting. Let us try something else." Mr. Sticks suggested. Mr. Stones, impassive as ever, just nodded.

They walked towards the back of the house, where there was an old bulkhead door that went into the cellar. This was less direct, and not ideal, but was Plan B. Mr. Sticks always had a Plan B, a Plan C, D and E. The door was secured by a stout, but rusty, padlock, Mr. Sticks pointed, and Mr. Stones reached down and took hold of the lock.

He squeezed slowly, and his large grey hand crushed the lock as easily as a grown man could crush a grape. He opened his hand and the mangled remains of the lock fell to the floor, he pulled back the clasp and wrenched open the wooden door. Beneath the door was a hole, which dropped down into darkness, wooden stairs disappearing downward, into darkness.

Mr. Sticks went first, taking a tentative step down, then another and another, down into the inky darkness. Then there was another scream and a few moments later a thud and some snapping noises. Mr. Stones shook his head in annoyance, a rare show of emotion, and peered in. Slowly as his age-old eyes became accustomed to the dark, he saw that the stairs stopped after the fourth one, and that there was a 15 foot fall to the floor beneath. Mr. Stones could just make out the thin figure of Mr. Sticks, lying still on the floor, his arms and legs bent in unnatural positions.

Mr. Stones shrugged and took the direct route down: he picked up the two bags, slung them over his shoulder and simply jumped. He thudded to the floor below moments later with a shuddering impact. The landing didn't even make his knees bend, if he had knees at all. He looked down, picked up Mr. Sticks by his neck and hoisted him off the ground.

"Pish posh, this house does not seem to welcome visitors, Mr. Stones, but we are in now. Give me but a moment to straighten myself out."

Mr. Sticks looked down at his legs, both bent at a 90-degree angle. Still being held by Mr. Stones, he reached down with his hands and wrenched one leg, then the other. There were several snapping sounds, and he grunted with the sensation. When his legs were mostly straight again, Mr. Stones placed him back on the ground.

"Hmmm, it appears we will have to watch our step, Mr. Stones. These little incidents are upsetting our timeline."

"WHERE NOW?"

"Up, Mr. Stones, we must go up. He is in the highest room in the tallest tower."

Chapter Seventeen

It's a bit of a myth that all vampyrs sleep in crypts, mausoleums and cellars. They do not need to be hidden from the sun, but the main thing they like is security. Cellars and the like tended to have one way in, and no other way out, and so are too easy to get trapped in. Sir Francis preferred to sleep in the highest room, as if all else fails to escape he can defenestrate himself. Falling out the window would hurt, but even in full daylight he could escape from any pesky vampyr hunters or torch-carrying mobs.

Mr. Sticks and Mr. Stones looked around, the cellar was dusty and low meaning Mr. Stones had to stoop to make his way through it. Mr. Sticks had no such problem. Cobwebs hung from the ceilings and small forms with long tails scuttled around at their feet. Over to their left was a set of wooden stairs leading up to the ground floor. They walked over, or rather Mr. Sticks scurried and Mr. Stones stomped, and reached the bottom.

Mr. Sticks was about to take the lead, but stopped, and stood back.

"Where are my manners, after you Mr. Stones," he smirked at his companion. Mr. Stones just stared blankly, and then started up the stairs.

He walked up the stairs slowly and inexorably, like the passage of a glacier creating a fjord. He leant from side to side, as he was not very flexible and so could hardly bend his legs. The whole process seemed to take an eternity, but then he was at the top. Mr. Sticks waited at the bottom of the steps, trying to expect the unexpected.

At the top of the stairs was a stout oak door. Mr. Stones went to grab the brass handle the door suddenly swung open, directly into Mr. Stones face. He was still slightly off balance from climbing the step, meaning the door did not bounce off him like it usually would. One foot was still off the floor, and he was leaning to one side.

The timing was perfect, the door caught him full in the face and knocked him backwards. He fell onto his back and slid down the stairs like a piece of furniture. He gathered speed and momentum quickly due to his weight, despite the stairs being quite short. He landed at the bottom with a thud, and the sound of cracking twigs and branches.

Unfortunately, or fortunately depending on your point of view, he had landed right on top of Mr. Sticks.

Mr. Stones sat up awkwardly, as bending was a problem, and clambered to hit feet and looked down.

On the floor was Mr. Sticks, or what was left of him. His brown suit had burst open at the seams from the impact, and his body could be seen - but it was not a normal human body. Instead, it was a network of twigs, branches, stems and shoots. They all normally had intertwined together to make roughly a human-like shape, but now they had all snapped and fractured and were scattered all over the floor. His face had half come off, showing a network of twigs beneath and the fake skin covering his mouth.

Mr. Stones listened closely and could hear a muffled sound from behind the fake face.

"Oh, darn it and blast it! Mr. Stones, look what has become of me, it will take some time for me to pull myself together. I would be most appreciative if you could look for a brush, so that you can sweep me up in a pile in the corner."

Mr. Stones looked around in the gloom and found an old yard brush leaning against the wall in a dusty corner of the room, next to a lumpy old mattress. He stomped over and grabbed it and started to sweep Mr. Sticks into a pile of twigs and branches, directly underneath his head.

ouch

Over the next few minutes something remarkable happened: the snapped twigs started to straighten and broken stems started to knit back together. Then they all started to pull themselves together under the strange head with its wonky face. First the chest and abdomen reformed, then the legs, then the arms.

Mr. Sticks got to his feet, naked he looked like a nude scarecrow, and looked at his ruined suit. He reverted to Plan C.

"This will never pass muster, Mr. Stones, can you find me my spare suit?"

Mr. Stones unzipped one of the black bags and rummaged around. Unable to immediately lay hands on Mr. Sticks' spare clothing, he stuck his head in the bag and leaned (as far as he could lean) into it. His huge frame was almost half inside the 2-foot-long bag when he grunted, possibly in triumph. He pulled himself back out with the last thing to emerge one of his huge hands clutching a coat stand. A six-foot-tall wooden coat stand, which he pulled out of the much smaller bag. On the stand was hanging a new brown suit.

Mr. Sticks quickly re-dressed, straightened his face, and then checked his hair. Except he did not, as it wasn't there.

"My hair!" he exclaimed, "where's my hair?"

He needed his hair, as his false face only covered the front, back and sides if his head. At the moment, it looked like he was wearing a nest as a hat, as a network of twigs sat atop his head, where the face finished - he would never pass as human without his hair.

They both looked around and it was Mr. Stones that spotted the pale wig. The impact had obviously caused it to be dislodged from Mr. Sticks head and was hanging from an old, broken wall light. Mr. Stone reached over, plucked it up and slapped it onto Mr. Sticks head, backwards. The back of the hair was now the front, and the front now the rear.

"Really, Mr. Stones. That will not do, not at all. Some care is needed in the placement."

He reached up with his twiggy fingers and spun the hair around, pushing it into place, until it clicked into place, like when a child would stick hair on a Lego figure.

"This really is becoming most tiresome, Mr. Stones, but onward and upward. We still have an assignment to complete, and we always complete our assignments."

Mr. Stones started up the stairs again.

Chapter Eighteen

Meanwhile across town, Mr. March sauntered to the High Street. He took a left turn and moseyed down a smaller street, near the town hall. He took a final right turn and meandered down a dark alley. He was, as usual, wearing his tweed suit and deerstalker, slung over his shoulder was a battered old leather satchel, with the letters "MM" monogrammed just above the lock in gold.

Mr. March never rushed anywhere, but today he had felt the need to. There was something wrong, something off - and he was worried. Mr. March never worried. He normally lived in the moment and never thought of consequences.

Today was different. Today, as he had seemingly just been sauntering, moseying and meandering, he had felt the need to run, but just in case he was being watched he could not take the risk.

He stopped under a faded wooden sign, that hung over some stone stairs down to a basement door. The sign said, or once said,
"CHARLES HOLLAND: ANTIQUE AND VINTAGE BOOK SHOP"

But the gold guilt lettering had faded and peeled off over time, so now it said:
"CHAR AND ANTI AGE BOO
HOP"

It was not a shop only selling books about the Netherlands, rather it was owned by a Mr. Charles Holland. Mr. March badly felt the need for Mr. Holland's advice and rather specialist knowledge.

Speaking of books, there is an old saying that is quite apt here. You should never judge a book by its cover, and this was particularly true of Mr. March. He may appear happy go lucky and to just float around oblivious to the world around him, but that is not the case.

Mr. March had very good senses and rarely missed anything - he had eyes as sharp as a cat, ears as acute as a bat, and a nose as sensitive as a rat. He had noticed two figures in Shackledown Road, two most unusual figures. The first was short and stick thin, and the second was large and grey, like a boulder wearing a suit. They seemed to be watching, always watching, but never watching Mr. March.

They seemed to be interested in the Bannerworth kids, and their comings and goings to Ratford House.

He ambled down the steps to the front door of this most unusual store. He had known Mr. Holland for a long time, a long, long time in fact. He looked around and seeing no one was watching (as there was no one else in the alley) he opened the door and slipped through.

A bell dinged as he opened the door, leading him to a small room. Well, it might have once been a large room, but it was so full of books that it was now a small room. There were books everywhere: small books, tall books, thick books and thin books. From great, big leather-bound tomes to slim volumes or pamphlets. The room was filled with floor to ceiling shelves and all these shelves were crammed, rammed and stacked with books. There were books on tables, piled high almost to the ceiling, and then there were just random piles of magazines on the floor. The room smelt of dust and old paper, a very musty yet pleasant smell.

At the back of the room there was a small counter, half stacked with books, and on the other half was a large ornate cash register. It was huge, green and gold, and looked as it if weighed a tonne - the last price rung up on it was in shillings and tuppence. To get to the counter was one path through the piles and stacks of books.

Mr. March successfully navigated his way through the piles of books and got to the counter. As he did, a figure emerged from a doorway behind the counter; a man, who appeared to be about 40 years old, but appearances can be deceptive. He had what one can only describe as a book-ish face. It was a face the looked as if it spent all its time reading, examining and cataloguing books.

On his narrow nose were a pair of pince nez glasses, the old-style ones with no arms that just seemed to cling to the bridge of his nose. His eyes were bright and inquisitive, but quite narrow set and he seemed to have a perpetual squint, his brow held thick lines from hours of concentrating on reading.

"Ah Mr. M" he exclaimed delightedly. His voice was dry, like the turning of a page. "It is Wodensday already? It is time for our weekly game?"

"Regrettably not, Mr. H. Today is only Moonsday, but something is afoot."

"Ah, I thought I had got lost in my days again."

This happened to Mr. Holland quite a bit, he could happily pick up a good book and get lost in its pages for days on end.

He continued, "Indeed, you look more perturbed, Mr. M. How can I be of service?"

"There are a couple of rum-looking fellows who seem to be taking an interest in my current lodgings."

"An interest? In you? Do you think they suspect?"

"No, Mr. H, they have an interest in the children."

"The, er...Bannerworths?" queried Mr. Holland. Mr. H never forgot a word he had read, but quite often forgot most things that had been said.

"Yes indeed," replied Mr. March, nodding his head in surprise that Mr. H had in fact remembered. "Very interested in the comings and goings of the children between No.99 and Ratford House."

"Ratford House?" enquired Mr. H, sounding vaguely surprised, "so has the resident of said house risen from his slumber?" Mr. Holland had read all about the resident of Ratford House.

"So, it appears Mr. H, so it appears."

"But you haven't seen him at all?"

"No, no, of course not, that would be very bad."

"Hmmm. Describe these fellows if you can, Mr. M."

"One looks like a scarecrow, if a scarecrow could walk. The other like a statue, if a statue could talk. I tried googling them but found nothing."

"Really Mr. M, your faith in modern methods is most disturbing", said Mr. Holland, a bit offended.

Mr. Holland did not like the internet. He thought that knowledge should be earned via books, and only using books to research; not by typing a phrase and clicking search and believing the first thing you find.

"Hmm, I think for this we will need to go to The Archives. Turn the sign and the latch Mr. M, we will need to go out back", Mr. Holland said The Archives as if it was capitalized, which it was.

Mr. March nodded and made his way straight to the door - well as straight as he could, which was not straight at all. He turned the sign in the door from 'open' to 'closed' and clicked the lock. Not that it would make any difference, as he had never seen anyone else in the shop, but Mr. Holland liked to do things his own way.

When he threaded himself back through the piles of books to the counter, Mr. Holland had already disappeared through the dark green curtain that half covered a doorless archway into the back of the shop. He silently cursed (although not really cursed, as curses are horrid things) Mr. H for not waiting. The last time he tried to find Mr. Holland in the back of the shop, he had gotten lost for 2 days - and Mr. March never got lost.

He pushed back the curtain, ducked under and made his way into the archives. Sorry, The Archives.

If the front of the shop was full of books, then The Archives were even worse. There were books everywhere, in piles and stacks, and different pathways seemed to lead off in various directions. Mr. March tried to smell his path through to Mr. Holland, but the dust made him sneeze. He sighed.

He walked down one corridor, then another and another. The Archives were immense and almost endless, how Mr. Holland had managed to cram a library larger than the British one into a small terrace basement, he would never know.

As indeed The Archives made the British Library look like a mobile library. The Archives contained a copy of every book ever written, and some that had not been. Eventually he got lucky and found Mr. Holland in a dusty row of reference books.

"Ah, there you are, I was concerned that you had gotten lost. Again." Mr. H said without looking up from a thick puce coloured volume, "I think I have found your odd fellows."

He held up the book. It was the Fellow Pages. Since time immemorial, if you needed a fellow to do a dodgy job, they could be found in the Fellow Pages. Its full title was incredibly long, but people just knew it by the term Fellow Pages. It did not just contain fellows, but women, boys and girls, humans and not, who for the right price would do any job for you.

"Here we are," said Mr. Holland pointing. The volume was about two thirds of the way open, and at the 'S' section. "I thought I remembered something."

Despite often not knowing if its Thorsday or Saturnsday, Mr. Holland never forgot something he had read, and never forgot where that book was in The Archives. Having to remember all that, it was hardly surprising he forgot other things.

He pointed at an advert, with a long, thin fingers. It was an oblong box on the page, close to the end of the S section:

STICKS AND STONES
WE BREAK BONES
MISS WORDS WILL
ALWAYS CHARM YOU
SPECIALISTS IN EXTRACTIONS, ELIMINATIONS
AND ERADICATIONS
CALL NOW – SPECIAL RATES
NO JOB TOO BIG

"Oh dear," said Mr. March "This is bad. I need to get back home, now."

He tore the page out of the Fellow Pages, removed his hat and folded the paper, tucking it inside the internal hat band. Without another word, Mr. March turned and ran back through the archives. He followed his own dusty footprints back to the front of the shop and dashed out the door.

Mr. Holland looked at the torn page, a bit annoyed with Mr. M for doing something so rude. But as he watched, the page started to re-appear bit by bit, until it was complete again. Mr. Holland closed the book and placed it back on its shelf.

Meanwhile, Mr. March was running. Mr. March rarely ran, but when he did, he could run very fast. He seemed to lope along the ground, eating up the distance in easy bounds - he raced along as fast as his legs could carry him.

For the first time for a long time, he was worried. No, that wasn't true, he wasn't worried, he was scared. Nope, still not right. He wasn't scared, he was terrified.

Chapter Nineteen

Back at Ratford House, Mr. Sticks and Mr. Stones had made some progress, but at some cost. The house continued to hamper at their progress: on the first floor, a ceiling had fallen in on them. Mr. Sticks had taken the brunt of it and once again found himself literally in pieces, he grumbled and groaned as he pulled himself together once more.

Later, on the second floor, the floorboards gave way under Mr. Stones. He fell, or more accurately, plummeted to the ground two floors below; landing like a tonne of bricks (which was quite a precise approximation of his weight). Even Mr. Stones, who seemed all but indestructible, felt a bit battered.

He was a bit chipped at the edges and had somewhere lost an ear and two fingers. Unlike Mr. Sticks, Mr. Stones was not able to regenerate as he was so hard to damage, it had never occurred to his maker to give him that ability.

After plummeting to the ground below, he had struggled back to his huge feet and shuffled back up the stairs, where Mr. Sticks waited impatiently.

"Really, Mr. Stones, some haste is required. As we waste time, the day passes with surprising alacrity."

Mr. Stones grunted and they continued up the landing - ahead of them was the final stairs, to the tallest room in the house, the turret room in the western corner. Sir Francis preferred the western corner so he could sense the exact moment the sun was about to set.

Straight ahead of them was the stairs, they were straight, but crooked, as the tops of the stairs slopped from left to right - or right to left. Atop the stairs was a dark oak door, embossed upon it was the crest of the Varney family, a blue field with a white cross and five blue stars. The irony of the coat of arms bearing a crucifix was not lost on Mr. Sticks, Mr. Stones did not care.

They made their way up the stairs carefully, this house had taught them caution, even Mr. Stones who more than most normally wanted to act, rather than think, first. However, they managed to arrive at the door without incident and pushed.

It creaked open into the room which, as expected, was in near darkness. It was pentagonal in shape, with the door in one of the five walls. On the other walls were tall windows that reached from floor to ceiling and back again. Each was shuttered and only a few streams of early afternoon daylight managed to creep through the slats. The floor was thick with dust, as if no one had walked on it in decades.

In the centre was a large four poster bed. Again, vampyrs do not tend to sleep in coffins - unless they want to impress visitors. Coffins tended to be claustrophobic, hard and uncomfortable. Would you like to go to sleep for 30 plus years on a hard wooden floor? Or even worse, half buried in earth and mud.

It was hard enough for a modern vampyr to look their best, as they could not check their appearance in a mirror. And so sleeping in earth made it that much harder, especially as black showed up all the mud, and vampyrs did like to wear black.

There were some modern vampyrs who had decided to go back to coffins, crypts and sleeping in dirt; as did a few of the OV's (Original Vampyrs), but most liked the comfort of a plush bed. This bed, however, was unlike anything you have likely seen. Its tall posts were made of ebony, its base mahogany, and between each of the post was a screen made of walnut and teak. These screens were each made of 4 panels that could be folded back, but at present they were closed - so that the occupant was completely encased in wood and, therefore, darkness.

"**FINALLY.**" grumbled Mr. Stones

"Indeed Mr. Stones, this has been a most arduous affair. Let us hope that from hereon in, we can expedite this extraction and be away from this vexatious house. Now, let us prepare."

Without further a word, Mr. Stones placed the two black duffel bags on the floor. He unzipped one of them and once more rummaged inside finding what he wanted quickly, as he had purposefully packed little in this bag. From the 2-foot-long bag, he hauled out an ebony box, about 6 feet long, and 2 foot wide, and a foot deep. It had lid that was hinged in silver, with silver locks and handles.

It was a coffin.

He opened the locks and threw back the lid, inside was lined in dark velvet.

Then he took out of the bag some silver chains and manacles, placing them carefully on the floor by the huge bed.

"DO WE PROCEED?"

"Yes, now is the time, Mr. Stones."

They walked over to the bed and stood, one by each post on the left-hand side. At a signal, Mr. Stones grabbed the first panel and folded the screen back. It clicked backward, until the whole of the left side was open.

They had expected a bed made of black satin sheets.

Something dark and gothic - something vampyric.

Instead, they found a nice and light space. The bed sheets were a white, crisp linen. The pillows were plump and downy, and there was a light duvet. The duvet cover pale yellow, and covered in pictures of flowers, as were the pillows. The whole thing was all rather Laura Ashley. In the centre of the bed was Sir Francis, his eyes closed, and looking almost peaceful in his unnatural slumber. He was wearing a white linen shift, never understanding why so many vampyrs choose to sleep in their night clothes. Three-piece suits were not the most comfortable bed attire.

In one of his long claw-like hands was a cheap paperback book, a Jackie Collins novel. Sir Francis loved to read for a while at morning before going to sleep, and he loved a good page turner. Despite having the complete works of Shakespeare and Dickens (all originals of course, some of the Shakespeare's were even signed by Mr. Bacon, the author), Sir Francis loved a good modern-day thriller or pot boiler. Being a vampyr, he has perfect night vision and did not need a night (or day) light.

Mr. Sticks and Mr. Stones wasted no time in grabbing the slumbering vampyr and dragging him off the bed. Sir Francis' eyes flew open, staring at them. His eyes were still green form the glood, and seemed to pull Mr. Sticks and Mr. Stones in. They could see pastures of green, green grass in the deep wells of those eyes, they could see paradise.

Mr. Sticks shook his head, breaking contact with the jade eyes.

"Beware, Mr. Stones, he is attempting to mesmerize you. Avert your gaze."

Mr. Stones dragged his eyes from the hypnotic stare of Sir Francis, reached up and covered the vampyrs eyes with his huge, now three fingered, hand. Sir Francis writhed and thrashed around for all he was worth. Sir Francis was stronger, supernaturally so, and easily the equal of 10 grown human men, but he was no match for the strength of Mr. Stones and the tenaciousness of Mr. Sticks.

FV

They manhandled the vampyr off the bed and into the coffin, managing to get a bag over the squirming vampyrs head and then manacled him by the hands and ankles with the silver locks and chains. They threw closed the lid, clicked on the locks, and they were done.

"Finally, Mr. Stones, the quarry is ours. Come, let us depart this unkind residence and take our employer his prize."

Mr. Stones picked up the now occupied coffin and managed to shove it back into the second black duffel back. It disappeared inside the impossibly small bag, which was then zipped up.

They made for the stairs and headed down. Carefully.

Chapter Twenty

Mr. March made it back to No.99. He was slightly out of breath, but quickly found his key and unlocked the door, running into the house. No one was home, but he checked the kitchen clock. It showed 2:50pm, and so the kids would still be at school and Mrs. Bannerworth at work.

He decided to go and check Ratford House, although he was none too keen on getting too close. He stalked up the road towards the house and slipped through the crooked gate and up the crooked path. He was at the door, about to open it, when he heard a noise from around to the left. He crept to the corner of the house and peered around. He saw Mr. Sticks emerging from the bulkhead door. He was looking rather pleased with himself, although he looked a bit ragged.

Mr. March hid behind a rather unattractive shrub and watched; Sticks seemed to be talking to someone out of view. He decided he would try to creep up to Sticks. Maybe if he could see what they were up to, then he could follow them and assess the risk to the children.

He crept closer and closer, and then his haste overcame his stealth, and he stepped on a twig, brittle and dry, so it cracked and snapped under his foot. Sticks turned and saw Mr. March.

Perturbed, Sticks turned to call his companion, and seeing no other option, Mr. March jumped at him. He knew he could never take down both of them together. Mr. March disliked violence, but when he did attack he attacked with a feral rage - like a wild animal.

His deerstalker hat fell from his head as he leaped. His bound took Sticks by surprise, and soon the smaller man was on the floor. He strove to restrain Sticks, but the thin, spindly man had a surprising strength - the strength of woods and trees, of earth and branches.

They were locked in a struggle, wrestling and rolling around on the floor - Mr. March started to lose control and felt his animal rage take over. His hazel eyes went a vivid yellow, and the pupils became slitted. His hands started to elongate and lengthen, becoming more claw like. His nails started to grow into long yellow talons, his nose started to grow outwards as did his mouth, turning into a snout. His teeth started to lengthen and become distinctly fang like, his ears becoming long and pointed.

Mr. Sticks screamed as he realised that he was overmatched, Mr. March continued to change, and all humanity left his face. His sideburns grew, his eyebrows became more prominent and bushier. The whole of his face was now covered in dark hair or, more accurately, fur. The visceral, primeval strength of Mr. March was winning. He pinned down Mr. Sticks, sat astride him and roared at him.

"What are you doing here? Why are you watching the children?" he howled in an animal, guttural voice.

Sticks looked terrified and was about to reply, but then a huge grey, three-fingered fist seized Mr. March by the collar and lifted him effortlessly off Sticks. Mr. March hung there, like a puppy in the mouth of his mother, dangling. He wriggled and kicked, but even his animal strength was nothing compared to the power of Stones. The strength of mountains and hills, of cliffs and boulders. Then Stones other hand came up, balled into a fist. It ploughed into Mr. March like an avalanche and knocked him unconscious. Mr. Stones, dropped Mr. March to the floor, were he lay in a crumpled heap.

Mr. Sticks got to his feet and dusted himself down, looked down at the half human, half animal figure of Mr. March, and said,

"Hmm, fascinating. We never suspected that. Still, there may be more revenue for us in this, Mr. Stones. Manacle the cur and bring him along, I am sure our employer will be interested. Otherwise, there will be some other kennel we can use to house this mutt."

Mr. Stones turned around and picked up the two bags he had dropped by the bulkhead door when he had seen Mr. Stick's predicament. He reached into the second bag, rummaging around, and found his spare sets of silver manacles. He fastened them wrist and ankle to Mr. March. As soon as the silver touched his flesh, Mr. March seemed to start to revert to a more normal shape and size.

Mr. Stones stuffed him into the first duffle bag, as the second was getting rather cramped for space, and slung them both over his shoulder. Mr. Stones did not see the deerstalker hat, as it had knocked off the path during the fight to be half-hidden by a bush.

"Let us make haste, Mr. Stones, to our employer's lair."

They walked off down the crooked path and through the crooked gate. But the fight with Mr. March had caused Mr. Sticks trousers to rip in the thigh. As he walked, every few steps, a twig, stem or leaf would fall from the rip onto the pavement.

Chapter Twenty One

It was now 3:15pm and the bell rang at school. The kids were positively on the edge of their seats for all their final lessons. As soon as the bell rang they were off, running out their classes, down to the bus stop.

As soon as they got home, as with any other day, they dropped off their bags, warmed up a cup of the glood, and ran around to Ratford House as soon as dusk fell.

They arrived at Ratford House, and opened the crooked gate, that was already open; they ran down to the crooked path and arrived at the crooked door. George was in the lead and grabbed at the brass doorknob.

However, the house was still being protective and didn't immediately recognise the kids (although the house really liked them) and there was a slight electric charge through the doorknob. George was thrown backwards, although he felt he was thrown forwards. He fell to the ground, his palm smoking slightly. He staggered back up to his feet and looked down at his slightly blackened palm - it hurt, but he tried to ignore it.

"Your hair!" cried Flora "it's all spiky! It's like when dad went to that 80's night and his hair stuck up on end."

George reached up and touched his hair. It was normally thick and dark brown but liked to stay close to his face. Now, his hair was spikey and stuck up, like a porcupine, or a blue hedgehog from one of his video games.

"I'm OK," said George, not that Flora or Henry had asked.
They were more interested in why he had a hair style like a member of Sigue Sigue Sputnik (whoever they were).

"That was so cool," chirped Henry "you flew through the air like a superhero!"

"Hmm, it didn't feel that way," replied George, "But I don't want to try the door again. Maybe Sir Francis is in the back garden? Let's go this way and see," George pointed to the right of the doorway.

George headed off towards the right of the door, Flora and Henry followed.

Around the corner they found a sash window - it was closed, but the paint had flaked off it and there were signs it had been forced. More telling were the stick-like fingers that were stuck, still trapped, under the window sill, wriggling and writhing.

George leaned in and examined them. He was a logical boy and liked logical solutions, but this provided him with none.

"Hmm," he murmured to himself "This makes no sense. It looks like those fingers, if they are fingers, are still alive."

The continued around to the back garden. On a line were a series of dark suits, and white ruffled shirts, hung out to dry in the winter dusk - but no sign of Sir Francis. They continued around the house and turned the corner and saw the bulkhead door open.

"How odd," said Flora.

"Indeed" said George. He could feel his detective powers starting to come to life. George loved Sherlock Holmes, Miss Marple and Father Brown, though he did, however, find Poirot very annoying.

"Look" cried Flora "isn't that Mr. March's silly hat?"

Under a bush was a battered, old deerstalker hat. It looked exactly the same as the old, battered deerstalker hat that Mr. March normally wore. George was a bit annoyed that he had not spotted it first.

"That is odd, Mr. March loves that hat." Said George, thinking out loud, "And it seems he was here, as he would never have left it behind."

"What's that poking out? It's a bit of paper" noticed Flora of the inside of Mr. March's hat. Again, George was irritated for a moment as he had missed it, but then felt proud of Flora as she was so observant.

George pulled the paper out, it was hurriedly folded so he straightened it out. It said,

STICKS AND STONES
WE BREAK BONES
MISS WORDS WILL
ALWAYS CHARM YOU
SPECIALISTS IN EXTRACTIONS, ELIMINATIONS
AND ERADICATIONS
CALL NOW – SPECIAL RATES
NO JOB TOO BIG

"Oh, this doesn't sound good." said George.

"What do we do, George?" asked Henry, slightly nervously.

"We go inside and try to find Sir Francis of course" replied George calmly. He did not feel very calm. "Come on, let's go inside."

They all looked down into the dark cellar, they could only see the first three steps down. Hand in hand, they took the first steps down into the cellar. Then the second, the third and the fourth. Then there was a cry and a yell - or three cries and three yells.

Chapter Twenty Two

It wasn't a long walk to their employer's lair, so they soon arrived. About a mile from Shackledown Road was an old retail park, it had suffered over the years and a lot of the units were empty and up for rent. In one of these, their employer had set up his lair. Yes, he really did call it his lair.

Mr. Sticks and Mr. Stones arrived at the front door. Above the door, a CCTV camera stared down at them curiously. CCTV cameras can only really stare, as they do not have eyelids and cannot blink. But they are not often curious. There was a red button on the wall next to the door which Mr. Sticks pushed with one twiggy finger.

"Yerrs" came a voice from a speaker above the button.

"It is Mr. Sticks and Mr. Stones. We have accomplished our assignment and seek admission and imbursement."

Imbursement was just another word for payment. Mr. Sticks and Mr. Stones were very keen on payment. It's not like they did these things for Scotch mist.

"Most excellent. Then enter, my friends."

Mr. Stones stared at Mr. Sticks "**FRIENDS?**" he grumbled.

"Strange concept, isn't it?" replied Mr. Sticks.

There was a buzzing noise and the door partly opened. Mr. Sticks pushed at it and the door fully opened inwards. They walked through the door, Mr. Sticks with ease though Mr. Stones more had to duck through it.

Inside was a large open plan room, or more like a warehouse. It was fully 200 metres long, and 100 metres wide. It was lit by long fluorescent bulbs that ran along the ceiling in parallel, various machines lined the walls of the room. But more of those later.

FV

A man walked to greet them; he was of medium height, and somehow managed to appear thin and fat at the same time. He had a slim body, but his head was round and bulbous and covered in wrinkles with a shock of grey hair that stuck up in whorls. He wore dark trousers and who knew what else, as the rest of him was covered in a long, white lab coat that was buttoned up to the top.

"Well, let us release our guest." said Professor Chillingworth. He walked over to a high-backed chair and sat down in it, for drama, he turned the back of it to Mr. Sticks and Mr. Stones.

"Mr. Stones, if you would be so kind." Mr. Sticks said.

Mr. Stones dumped down the two duffel bags, one on the floor and the other on the table, unzipping the one on the table. He hauled the ebony coffin out of it, unlocked the locked locks and pulled open the lid. He picked up the body inside and hauled it out of the coffin and pulled the black bag off the figure's head.

Sir Francis blinked several times in the bright light. He did not really need to blink, but he felt it was appropriate for the dramatic circumstances of the situation.

Chillingworth spun round in his chair to face Sir Francis - it was a shame he hadn't remembered to have a white cat on his lap, he thought.

"Ahh, finally, Sir Francis Varney, welcome to my lair. I've been expecting you."

"Lair?" questioned Sir Francis "Is this not the old retail park just off the A616?"

"Well, yes, but what did you expect?" said Chillingworth, slightly deflated.

TO DO LIST
GET WASHING
BUY A WHITE CAT
CAPTURE A
VAMPIRE
VAMPYR
BECOME IMMORTAL

“

"A hollowed-out volcano? A private island surrounded by man eating sharks?" suggested Sir Francis "Is this not the old Toys-R-Us store?"

"No, it's not." replied Chillingworth, somewhat churlishly.

"Yesssss it is, look – there is an old sign above the door" he pointed at it with his chin.

Over the front door was a yellow sign with a multicolored logo and a cartoon picture of a giraffe, saying 'Thank you for shopping at Toys R Us. Please call again'.

"Look, do you know how hard it is to find a dormant volcano in greater London?" protested the Professor, clearly upset.

"Yesssss, but it is just a case of style. If you are going to call it a lair, could not you have found a derelict church or perhaps an old house?"

"Look, I was on a budget. Anyway, as I was saying, we meet again."

"Erm, again?" queried Sir Francis, "I am afraid I have never seen you in my life."

"You must remember me; I am your antagonist, your opponent, your advisory."

"No, sorry" replied Sir Francis, rather embarrassed.

The problem with having such a long life was that it was often difficult to remember faces from the past. That is why it was often easier just to drink them. He didn't have a clue who this round faced man was, and in spite of his precarious position, he felt a bit sorry for him.

"But you must know me! We have fought for over 60 years. I found you in that loft in Prague in 1972?"

"Oh, that was you? I thought it was a much younger fellow."

"But I was much younger then!" cried Professor Chillingworth.

"Hmm, good point, I will give you that," Sir Francis often forgot that humans tend to age. And at an alarming rate.

"Then again in that cellar in Barcelona in 1975."

"You again? Really? Well, I must say you are most tenacious."

Sir Francis was a bit peeved that someone had mentioned he was living in a cellar. He really did find it very stereotypical of vampyrs to be found in a cellar of all places. But he was on a gap "year" traveling around Europe at that time, and sometimes you just had to stay anywhere. Hostels, yurts, and even cellars. Still, what a gap year it had been, so much so that it actually lasted 40-odd years.

"Yes, for I am your nemesis, Professor Chillingworth."

"Chillingworth you say? Well, I do sort of remember a student called Chillingworth when I was in Paris. In the 1960's?"

"Yerrs? Continue."

"Bit of a creep I seem to recall. Begged me to turn him, but I never wanted to be a father, or a sire. Never wanted the responsibility, I was only 750 and was not ready for kids or settling down. And if I had, if I had to turn anyone it would not have been him - he was really . . ." Sir Francis stopped for a moment. And then continued "Oh, was that you?"

Chillingworth stared at him, rather chillingly.

"Oh, my apologies." said Sir Francis.

"Yes, I was in Paris," cried Chillingworth, "and since then I have hunted you like a cat hunts a rat."

"Really? Do cats hunt rats? I thought they tended do stick to mice. Rats are quite big, you know."

"Well, like a dog tracks a-" replied Chillingworth.

"Hog?"

"Why did you say hog? A dog doesn't hunt a hog. That absurd," said Chillingworth, irritated.

"My humblest apologies, I thought you liked the rhyming thing. Cat, rat. Dog, hog. You can see how I got confused."

"Well, be that as it may, I have found you now and captured you," Chillingworth almost screamed in anger. "You are mine, Sir Francis, and you will regret not turning me all those years ago."

"I would calm down if I were you," suggested Sir Francis. "You seem to be getting very irate, it is not good for your heart. It has shot up to 140 BPM in the last few minutes."

Sir Francis may not have drunk a human for some time, but he could still sense their heart rate. And from the smell of him, Professor Chillingworth was AB negative. Tasty! Old habits die hard.

"My heart is fine, thank you. Or shall I say it will be soon." Screamed Professor Chillingworth. He turned and pointed at Mr. Sticks and Mr. Stones.

"Take him to The Machine"

Chapter Twenty Three

The kids fell down towards the hard packed earth of the cellar floor, a full 15 feet below. As with Mr. Sticks, they had missed the fact the stairs stopped at the fourth one down. They fell, whirling their arms as if they were trying to fly. But they had no talent in flying, they fell - and they were very good at falling. They were only a couple of feet above the ground, if they hit then they would be hurt at least. At worst…well that could be bad, very bad.

Luckily Ratford House realised that it had made a mistake. It had been shocked by the intrusion of Mr. Sticks and Mr. Stones, and it wasn't quite feeling itself. It liked the kids and really didn't want them to come to any harm so a lumpy old mattress that was in the corner of the cellar all of a sudden moved under the children. Just in time! They landed on the plump mattress and huffed as the air was forced from their lungs.

George was first to his feet.

"Everyone OK?" he asked.

Flora and Henry cried out "yes" and jumped up, and they all hugged each other in relief.

"Where now?" asked Flora.

"Up" said George, "the only way is up."

In the gloom of the cellar, they found the steps up to the ground floor. At the base of these steps, George said:

"Stop, look at this."

At the base of the stairs was a suit - an old brown suit. Or what remained of it. The suit had split at all the seams, as if a massive weight had hit it from above. There was nothing in the suit, but around it were twigs, leaves, branches and stems.

"How odd" said Flora "it almost looks like a man was in that suit but was squished."

"Hmm" said George "stranger and stranger."

"Isn't it curiouser and curiouser?" asked Henry. He loved that book, in his view it could only have been improved with the inclusion of trucks and diggers - Henry loved trucks and diggers.

"It's not like we are in Wonderland now," said Flora.

They headed up the stairs to the ground floor.

Ratford House was a big, rambling house. It had many corridors and walkways, twists and turns. When the children arrived at the ground floor, Henry whispered,

"Look, what's that?" pointing at the floor.

On the floor was what looked like a stone finger and a stone ear, Flora bent down and picked them up. They were slightly warm, in a cold way.

"Strange," said George.

They carried on. After that it seemed like something was trying to direct them; doors would open unaided, lights would flicker and seem to point in a direction. They followed these signs, not doubting the familiar house.

They soon arrived at the last set of stairs, both straight and crooked, up to a door with a coat of arms on it. They dashed up the stairs, not afraid, and opened the door.

Inside they found a large four poster bed, but the bed was empty, except for a Jackie Collins paperback book. The sheets were rumpled and crumpled and there were signs of a struggle. At the end of the bed was a mannequin with Sir Francis' night clothes neatly placed on the human form.

"Hmm" said George, adopting his best Sherlock Holmes pose - it added to the image that he had picked up Mr. March's deerstalker hat and had decided to wear it.

George examined the floor. It was mostly thick with dust, but there were footprints, two different sets made by two different beings. The first set were small and pointed, the second large and square. By the left side of the bed was an imprint in the dust of a large oblong box, at least 6 foot long. Between the box and the bed were scuffled footprints and what looked like the shape of maybe a body being dragged along the floor. Aside from the dust, there were a few twigs and stems scattered on the floor.

"There has been a great struggle," proclaimed George. "It seems like someone has broken into here, or more accurately two someones, and maybe kidnapped Sir Francis."

"Can you kidnap a vampyr?" queried Flora.

"Yeah, surely you can only kidnap a kid?" said Henry in support.

"Well, it's just a turn of phrase."

"How do you turn a phrase?" asked Flora, puzzled.

"Well OK, someone has vampnapped Sir Francis. Is that better?" asked George, slightly exasperated.

Flora and Henry conferred for a moment, whispering between themselves.

"How about vampyrhended?" suggested Flora. Henry nodded in agreement although he really didn't know what the difference was, he usually tended to agree with whatever Flora had come up with.

"Fine, vampyrhended Sir Francis. Either way he is gone," replied George.

"So, what do we do now?" asked Flora.

George paced across the room, his hand to his chin in deep thought. It was something he had seen in various murder mysteries', and so he assumed it must help the thought process somehow.

"What do we know?"

"Not much," chimed Henry.

"No, we do, think!" replied George, a bit irritated "First we found the door alarmed against intrusion. Second we found the door to the cellar open." Like any good detective, he ticked them off on his fingers as he spoke.

"Third, we found Mr. March's hat. He has been here today, as he was wearing it this morning at breakfast."

Mrs. Bannerworth was always a bit annoyed that Mr. March insisted on wearing his silly hat at the breakfast, lunch or dinner table.

"Fourth, we found that empty suit at the bottom of the stairs in the cellar.

"And the twigs," added Henry.

"Yes, the twigs as well," agreed George, secretly impressed with Henrys memory, "Next, we found the house seemingly trying to point us in the right direction."

"Then we found a struggle in Sir Francis bedroom!" interrupted Flora.

"Indeed, we did. And what else did we find?"

"Sir Francis's clothes?" asked Henry.

"His rather dodgy taste in books?" mentioned Flora.

"No! What was on the floor? Aside from the scuff marks in the dust?"

"Twigs and branches," shouted Flora and Henry in unison.

"Exactly. We must make our way back outside. Now!" confirmed George.

They ran down from the highest room in the tallest tower, back to the cellar, and out through the bulkhead door - the stairs had somehow miraculously reappeared.

Looking around with new eyes, they saw the signs of a struggle outside and the huge square footprints in the mud next to the path. These footprints walked off down the crooked path, which was half mud. The kids followed them, but they disappeared when they got out of the crooked gate onto the solid pavement.

However, to the left of the gate was a twig, then a few feet later - a shoot. A few further feet on, a branch. Henry bent down and picked up a twig causing it to wriggle and twist in his hand. He yelped and dropped it.

"We must follow the wriggly twigs. The game is afoot," cried George, looking every inch the detective despite the oversized deerstalker hat that half covered his face.

Chapter Twenty Four

Back at Professor Chillingworth's lair, (or more accurately the old Toys-R-Us store on the retail park off the A313), Sir Francis found himself grabbed by each arm and walked towards one of the many different machines in the large room. Now he had time to study his surroundings, he realised it was some sort of laboratory. He had never been very good at science as when he was at school people still believed in magic and witchcraft.

However, he recognised a bench full of test tubes, conical flasks, and Bunsen burners. Another desk has a purple-coloured liquid in a large round bottomed flask, suspended by a clamp and gently bubbling away over a flame. Over the top of the flask was an inverted funnel that caught all the vapour that was being produced and fed them through an intricate complex of clear glass tubes.

Sir Francis was walking, or more being walked, towards a sort of X shaped bench. He realised struggling against the strength of Mr. Sticks and Mr. Stones was pointless and so decided to save his strength - with no idea when, or if, he would next get some glood from the kids, he may become weak if he exerted himself too much.

When they got to the bench, Mr. Stones held Sir Francis firmly whilst Mr. Sticks rolled up both Sir Francis' sleeves making him look like a Victorian dad on holiday. Mr. Stones lifted him onto the bench - the centre of the X was long enough to fit his body, each of his limbs were tied to an arm of the X. This meant he was lying there, bound and unable to move, as though he was in the middle of a star jump.

After he was securely strapped down, Professor Chillingworth approached and leaned over him.

"As you can see, Sir Francis, time has not been as kind to me as it has to you. But I mean to change that, for years I have theorised how a vampire- "

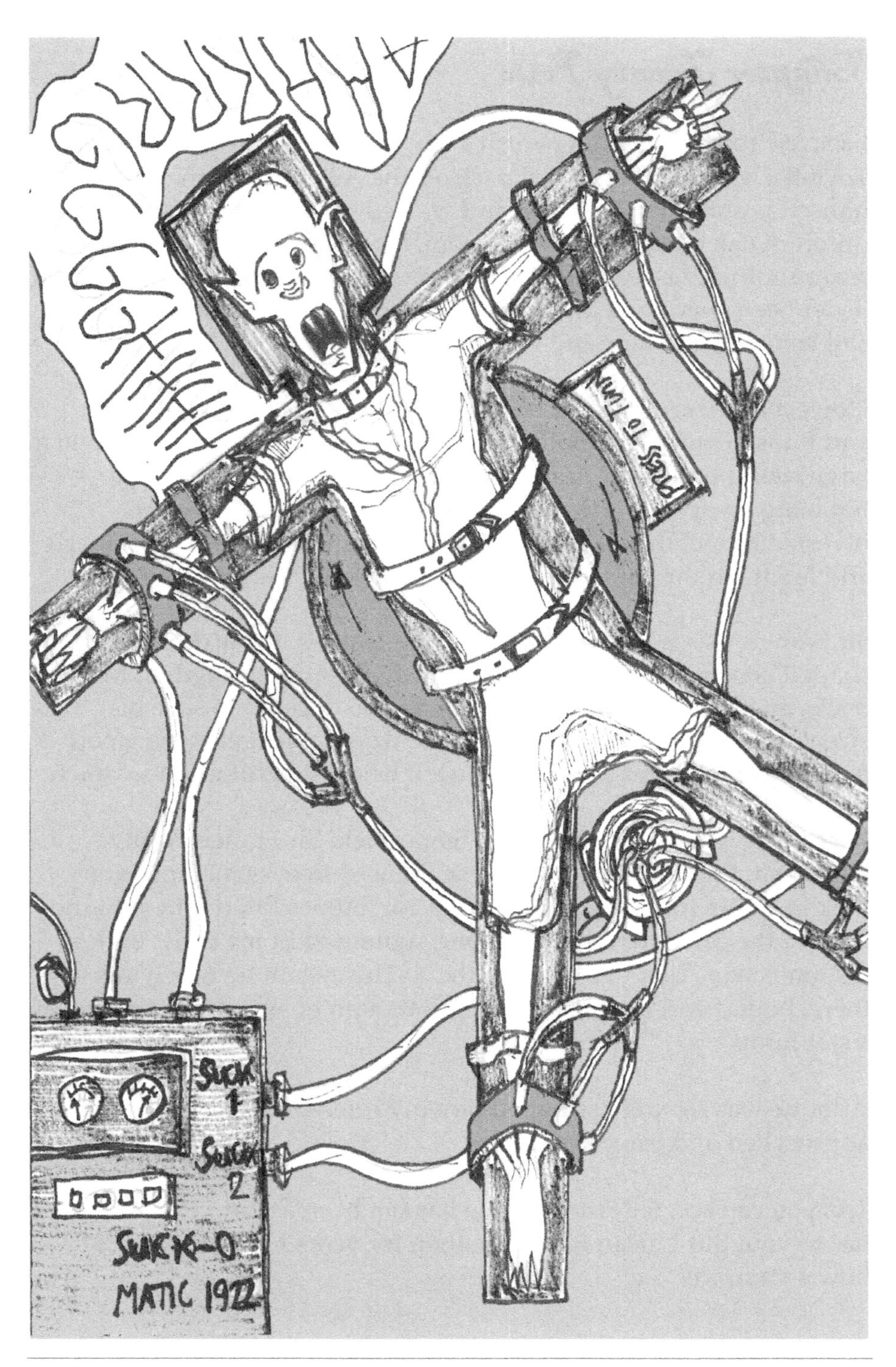

AARRRRGGGGHHHH
Press To Turn
SUCK 1
SUCK 2
SUCK-O MATIC 1922

"Vampyr, rhymes with sphere," interrupted Sir Francis, automatically.

"Hm, vampyr then, I have theorised how a vampYR has survived for centuries without aging - today I am going to put my theory to the test. Sadly, Sir Francis, it is highly unlikely you will survive the process, but sacrifices must be made to further scientific knowledge."

"Scientific knowledge? Professor, now, do not tell lies - you are not doing it for scientific knowledge. You are doing it so that you can live forever," accused Sir Francis.

"Well, if happenstance would have it that I happened to benefit from my experiments, why shouldn't I?" retorted the Professor, sneeringly. "But be that as it may, unfortunately you may find this rather painful."

Next to the bench was a panel of switches, knobs, buttons and dials. The Professor flicked a couple of red switches and four lights came on.

"From here, I am going to get my machine to put some needles into your arms and legs, near where the veins and arteries should be. My machine will then slowly extract all the life out of you in the form of an elixir that will collect here."

The Professor pointed to a large glass jar that was at the end of the bench behind him, Sir Francis had to take his word for he couldn't twist his head to see it.

"I just need the machine to charge up, that will take about half an hour, and then we can proceed."

"Good," grumbled Sir Francis "Anything is better than listening to you talk."

The Professor looked slightly annoyed and even upset by that but said nothing.

He turned back to the control panel and turned a couple of knobs to the right, the needles of two dials above them quivered up into a red zone on the dial's readout. The machine started to hum gently, and Sir Francis could feel that power thrumming through the bench he was so firmly attached to.

"So, Mr. Sticks, I understand you had a little extra for me?" asked the Professor of the small, shifty man.

"Indeed, good sir. Mr. Stones, please escort our other guest into the room."

Mr. Stones leant down, well nearly, and unzipped the other duffle bag, reached in and plucked Mr. March out by the collar of his, now slightly torn, tweed suit. He was still manacled in silver, and looked like Mr. March did every other day of the week rather than a wild beast.

"This animal tried to help Sir Varney as we were extracting him. He became quite feral and wild and so Mr. Stones had to restrain him; he seems to have something of the wild beast inside him."

The Professor walked up to where Mr. March was dangling from Mr. Stones grasp. He looked closely, bringing his face right up to Mr. Marchs', and staring him in the eye.

"Oh, indeed Mr. Sticks - this mutt may be very useful. There is a silver cage over to the right, if you can lock him in there then that would be greatly appreciated."

"Ah but first, Professor, what value would you place on such a creature?"

Asked Mr. Sticks, always keen to maximise their profits.

"Hm, a quarter as much again?" suggested the Professor.

"Double?" countered Mr. Sticks.

They haggled for a while, until they agreed on a price which was about a third more than what they were already getting paid.

"Very well, Professor. I just need a signature here," Mr. Sticks pulled out a long vellum sheet of paper and a feather quill from his inside jacket pocket.

Chillingworth signed it.

"And here, here and here please. We have to cross the lies, don't we?"

Chillingworth signed again and again and again, Mr. Sticks smiled and rolled up the manuscript and put it back in his inside pocket.

Mr. Stones carried Mr. March over to the cage, unlocked the manacles and threw him inside. He slammed the door and turned the lock. Mr. March lay there, still slightly stunned.

After about another 20 minutes there was a steady beeping noise from the machine.

"Righto. We are ready to go to work, Sir Francis. You may feel a little prick, or more exactly, several."

The Professor pressed some more buttons, flicked some more switches and turned some more knobs. Where the pale flesh of Sir Francis arms and legs were exposed, several needles appeared out of the machine, and started to position themselves in circles around his wrists and ankles. The needles started to move towards the (mostly) white skin of Sir Francis.

"Here we go Sir Francis, it's time to begin."

He pressed one more button and the needles started to pierce Sir Francis' undead flesh. He screamed.

Chapter Twenty Five

In Shackledown Road, the children decided what do to. They were sure that both Sir Francis and Mr. March had disappeared, possibly vampyrhended and man-napped respectively.

"Well," said George "we can't leave Sir Francis and Mr. March to whatever nasty fate that's in store for them. We are duty bound to help, do we all agree?"

"Yes!" Cried out Henry.

"Of course!" shouted Flora.

"Then let's be away, we have a trail to follow. I think that these twigs and branches are linked to this Sticks and Stone advert that Mr. March had in his hat. Let's follow the trail and see where it takes us. We must be careful, whoever can spirit away a vampyr will be tricky."

They started off down Shackledown Road, finding first a twig, and then a few feet down, a small branch. This continued as they left Shackledown Road and headed towards the outskirts of town. They knew this area well, as the school bus took them down this route. It took them about half an hour to get to the industrial estate, following the trail of twigs and leaves.

The estate used to be busy and all the units full, but over the years it had become half empty, a bit of a ghost town. The trail took them into the estate and down a couple of roads, then they were in front of an old unit that had a giant wooden "TO LET" sign in front of it, hammered into the grass verge. Someone trying to be funny had drawn a capital "I" in black marker pen between the "O" and the "L". Henry and Flora fell around laughing when they saw this, despite the seriousness of their mission. George just smiled and shook his head.

The trail stopped at the front doors.

EXIT
TOILET

"This must be the place," said George, murmuring quietly.

"Do you think this is the villain's lair?" asked Henry.

"Well, if it is, it's not very lair-ish, is it?" said George.

"Yes, I would have really expected somewhere a bit more dramatic. Isn't this the old Toys-R-Us store?"

"Yes, it's very disappointing. I had hoped when I first went to a villain's lair it would be an old castle or something." agreed George.

"Look, there are lights on inside!" said Flora in a quiet voice, pointing.

"Are we going to sneak in?" whispered Henry in a voice that was just as loud as his normal voice, which was pretty loud indeed.

Flora put her finger on her lips and said,

"SHHHUUUSSSHHH!" so loudly she sounded like a steam train.

George pulled the close and into a little huddle, away from the door. As quiet as he could, he said

"We can't go straight in; we need to see what's happening first. We could walk into a right pickle otherwise."

The unit had an oblong front. The bottom half was brick and the top half glass, but the windows were all frosted. In the centre were a set of double doors made of clear glass, but they had blinds pulled down on the inside so the kids couldn't see anything. Pale yellow light gleamed through the frosted glass in the dark early-evening.

"This is no good. We will have to try around the side," stated George.

They crept around the side of the building. There was a short road, presumably for deliveries to the back of the unit. They crept down it and found nothing, but at the back was a small car park. In the back of the building was a tall metal door, the sort that rolls up to allow trucks in. Henry was excited, as he thought that there may be a truck inside. Henry really liked trucks - and diggers.

The metal door was closed, but just to its right were some steps up to a back door. Around the back door were cigarette ends, litter from chocolate bars and burger takeaway wrappers. The door was also metal, but it was ajar by a crack with very little light spilling through.

"That's our best chance," said George, "it looks quite dark in there, so we may be able to sneak in and see what that is. Are you both ready?"

Flora and Henry glanced at each other nervously, but then nodded in unison, despite the fear in their eyes. George had never been prouder of them.

"Henry, you're the smallest."

"Only coz I'm the youngest!" protested Henry "and Mum thinks one day I will be taller than you George. She measured me when I was two!" he said proudly. Henry did not like to think of himself as being the smallest.

"Not now Henry," chided Flora gently "but you are the best at sneaking, aren't you?"

"Yes" confirmed Henry, looking pleased with himself.

"Henry, we will all go up to the door and I will peek in. If it is safe, can you sneak in and try to see anything? Make sure you aren't seen by anyone, have you got your felt tip pens and notebook?

Henry nodded and reached into his backpack. He always had his felt tips with him, and a small notebook, so he could practice drawing tractors. Henry also liked tractors.

"Do you think you can draw a plan of the room if you can see anything? Just a quick sketch."

"Yes, I can," said Henry, nodding enthusiastically.

"Flora, can you be look-out?" George asked.

"Yes!" Flora enjoyed being a look-out, and she rarely missed a thing.

"Great. You stay near the corner but out of sight and see if there's anyone coming. If you spot anyone, can you hoot like an owl?"

"Of course. Or I could tweet like a budgie, or caw like a crow, or-"

"An owl will be fine, thank you, just make sure you aren't seen. Right, here we go."

Flora deployed herself over the other side of the access road, as there were some large wheelie bins there that she could hide behind and see the access road and the car park at the back. When she was in place, she raised her hand and he finger and thumb were in the universal symbol for "OK".

"It's up to us now Henry. Let's go"

George and Henry crept up the short outside staircase to the metal door. George peaked around - the room inside was quite small, and quite dark, but he could see a few tables and chairs, a kettle and a fridge, and a sink. It must have been the break room for when the unit was in proper use, a little bit of light spilled through from another door at the far end of the room.

He pointed to Henry's book, and Henry passed it over and gave him a black felt tip. George paged through the book, past drawings of Massey Fergusons and John Deeres, until he found a blank page. He quickly sketched the layout of the room he had seen, and marked an "X" and whispered to Henry, giving his book and pen back.

"Go to this point and draw what you can see. But while you are drawing, count to 30. When you get to 30-"

"I can count higher than 30!" replied Henry with quiet pride.

"I know you can, but I only want to you to stay there for about 30 seconds"

"Oh, I see."

"And when you get to 30, sneak back here. Got it?"

"Roger that," And without a further word, Henry crept in through the door.

Just as he did, there was a blood curdling scream from within.

Chapter Twenty Six

In the large warehouse, Sir Francis screamed. The Machine had lots of little needles digging into his arms and wrists, below the skin, and they were sucking. They were sucking all the liquid, the vitality, the life out of him in bursts every few minutes. The jar at the bottom of the X shaped bench was filling up with a thick green liquid.

In between the bursts of suction, he reflected this was what it must feel like to be drunk. Not drunk like human adults did on beer, but how it must have felt for humans when he drunk them. He was not surprised a lot of them had screamed.

"*If I ever survive this,*" he thought, "*Then I promise I will not go back to drinking people*"

But then the Machine started sucking again and Sir Francis stopped thinking, and started screaming.

"Interesting," said the Professor, still standing at the control panel. Flicking switches and turning knobs. He walked over to the bench, and spun it round, as it was a bit like a dentist's chair that could swivel around. For the first time, Sir Francis could see the rear of the building.

"I had rather expected the liquid to be red, like blood. But green? Why should that be? Have you changed your diet recently?"

Sir Francis was too busy screaming to reply.

"Still, my science is sound. I am sure that whatever has kept you alive, or undead, for all these centuries will still aide me."

Sir Francis thrashed around and tried to pull at the straps that were restraining him, but he was getting too weak. He barely had the strength of two adult humans as it was.

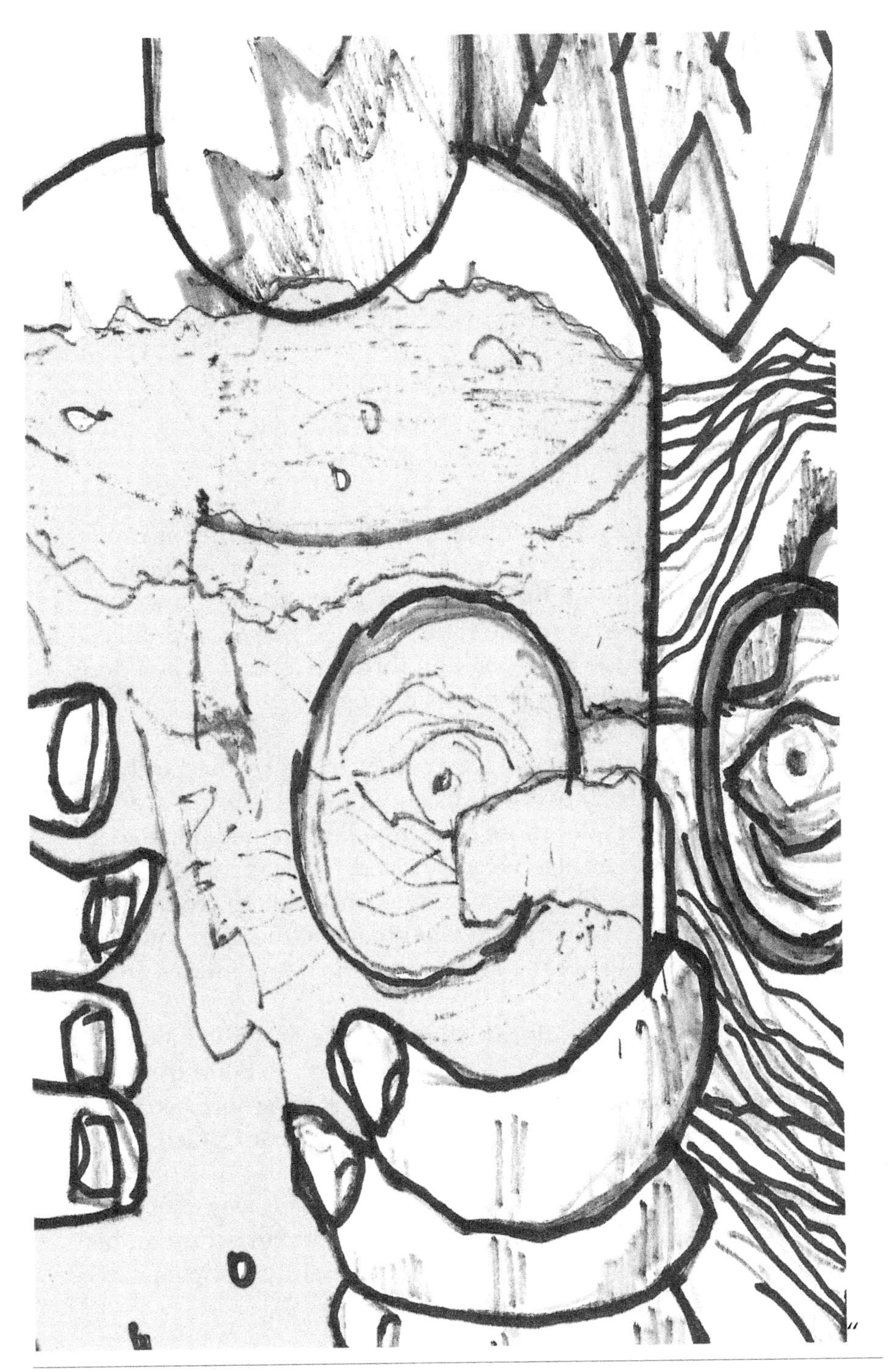

Hmmm, about a third of the way done I should think." said the Professor. "Maybe I should increase the flow and speed the process up?" he said to himself. "No, not for now. There's no hurry. Best get it right first time."

The Machine stopped sucking, and Sir Francis had a chance to get his breath. Not that he needed to, but some habits die hard. He looked around, turning his head, and for the first time, he saw that at the back of the room was a silver cage. In the cage was a familiar figure.

"Well I never" he said quietly "after all these years, is that Ma.....AARRGGGHHHHHH"

But the machine had started again, extracting more life, or unlife, from his thin and increasingly frail body. Sir Francis' eyelids fluttered and then closed. But just before they did, he glanced around the rest of the room. He rather fancied he saw a small round face, with white blonde hair, peaking through a partly open door. He smiled faintly, and then feinted, smilingly.

At the other side at the back of the room, Mr. March had fully recovered and was fully awake. His snout felt a bit bruised and would probably hurt a lot more next time he changed. He had a dull headache, and was also very annoyed. The cage was only waist height to a grown person, and so he was only able to crouch down. He put his hands on the bars and tried to rattle the door, but it was locked solid. He could see the keys on a table a few metres away.

The bars of the cage were also thick and made of white metal. Even in his other form he wouldn't be strong enough to bend them. He saw the occupant of the bench in the centre of the room, as it had now been spun around so he could see the occupant,s face.

The children had been right. He had awoken, as it was a face he knew very well, and he had spent many a night curled up on his bed whilst Sir Francis read a book (usually by Jilly Cooper) in the parlour of Ratford House.

Maximus Marchdale looked around the rest of the room. Professor Chillingworth, who he vaguely remembered when Mr. Stones had dragged him out of the duffel bag, was busy at the control panel next to Sir Francis. Sticks and Stones were just standing, watching, with their backs turned to him.

He glanced around, looking to see if there was anything he could reach to try to get the keys of the desk. An old brush, a mop, anything with a long handle would do. There was nothing. The only thing he could see was a portable pressure washer, with a long coiled hosepipe, attached to a tap on the rear wall. If only he could get the hosepipe but it was too far away. He looked around the rest of the room, along the back wall, and his eyes fell on a face. A face with blue eyes and a mop of blonde hair.

Chapter Twenty Seven

Henry had just got to the inside door when the screaming had started. He nearly jumped out of his skin, which would have been a neat trick. But he held his nerve and stayed at the door, and started drawing and counting. He saw the bench with Sir Francis on it, writhing and screaming intermittently, and drew it as quick as he could.

"4, 5, 6," he counted to himself.

He then saw the man at the control panel, who seemed to be talking to Sir Francis, when Sir Francis wasn't screaming and drew him.

"9, 10, 11,"

Then he saw the two strange figures of Mr. Sticks and Mr. Stones, who just stood watching. He drew them as best he could, and they looked a lot like a scarecrow and a statue from Easter Island.

"17, 18, 19,"

He glanced back at Sir Francis, who had stopped screaming, and their eyes met, briefly. Sir Francis smiled faintly at him and then his eyes closed. He looked dreadful. Well, maybe it would be better to rephrase that as he always looked dreadful. But he looked tired, and stick thin, and his eyes were dull and lifeless, even more so than normal.

"25, 26, 27,"

Then he turned and looked and saw the cage.

"Mr. March" he mouthed in amazement. Mr. March stared back at him, and gestured to the table, and mimed unlocking a door.

"28, 29, 30."

OUTSIDE I THINK

Doors

SCIENCE STUFF (dunno)

BIG SCARY MAN

A MACHINE THAT SUCKS

OUCH!

I hate school

SCIENCE GUY

(don't like HIM)

Cake

NOT SO SCARY MAN

SIR FRANCIS

KEY

WHERE'S Flora?

Mr Marsh

door

ME

I'M A HERO!

BY HENRY Age 6 1/4

Some Machine

(MAY BE USEFUL LATER)

GEORGIE

Henry nodded and sneaked back away from the door, back to George and Flora.

George was waiting at the outside door as Henry crept out.

"I made that 32 seconds Henry, but good work. Did anyone see you?"

"Yes," Henry replied, and George looked concerned "but no one bad."

George signaled Flora who returned back to the steps and they all looked at the plan Henry had drawn. Henry explained exactly what he had seen.

"So there's three of them, and three of us. Those two over there," George pointed at the scarecrow and statue, "I imagine are these Sticks and Stones fellows. I don't know who that man is by Sir Francis."

"He looked like a doctor, or a scientist," said Henry, "He was wearing a long, white coat like scientists do"

"There may be three of them and three of us," said Flora, "but they are a lot bigger than us"

"Yes we need help. It seems they are busy with Sir Francis, although it sounds like he doesn't have much time left. So we can't go for help, or we will be too late."

"But they aren't looking at Mr. March" said Henry, "he's just locked away in the cage."

"So if we can free Mr. March...." thought George thinking aloud, "Then he can help us. Show me again, what did he do when he saw you?"

"Mr. March? He pointed at a table nearby and then did this."

Henry did the same mime that he had seen.

"The keys" said Flora excitedly "he's telling us the keys to the cage are on the table."

"So that's our first priority. We have to get those keys and free Mr. March."

"We need a division." said Henry.

"A diversion you mean?" corrected Flora.

"Yes, a diversion." Henry replied.

"Good idea" said George "I think I have a plan. Flora, you have the best aim. Take these."

George picked up a few pebbles from the side of the road and handed them to Flora.

"Go around the front, and when I give the signal, throw them at the windows, but find somewhere to stay out of sight."

"The sign at the front, the TO(I)LET sign." Flora suggested.

Henry giggled. That was still very funny.

"Ideal, duck behind there, stand up, throw a stone and hide, then keep doing that until you see movement, and then just hide"

"OK, got it. What's the signal? Hoot like an owl?"

"No I can't do an owl, I'll caw like a crow" said George.

"What am I going to do?" asked Henry.

"When Flora has their attention, they should all look to the front of the building. You go and wait at the inside door again, and watch the people. When they are too busy wondering what all the noise is, you sneak in as quickly as you can, grab the keys and get them to Mr. March. Then get out"

"OK."

"I'll wait outside, and when Henry is back out, I'll coo like a dove. If it's safe, you come back around here Flora and we will work out our next move," said George "any questions?"

Flora and Henry shook their heads.

"Right, not a moment to waste. Let's do this."

George held out his hand, and Flora put hers on his, and Henry laid his on top of Flora's. They had seen this an old film. Something to do with muskets and swords. Then they raised their hands into the air and separated.

Flora ran off to the front of the building and crouched down behind the TO(I)LET sign. Henry crept back in and waited at the inside door. George stayed at the steps, and took a deep breath and raised his head, wrapping his hands around his mouth to form a tube. George cawed like a crow.

Chapter Twenty Eight

The plan worked. Mostly.

After George cawed, then Flora jumped up from behind the TO(I)LET sign end threw a stone. Her aim was true, and it hit one of the windows, not breaking it, but making a satisfying cracking sound. She ducked back down and waited a few moments and then threw another. Then another.

Inside, Henry was waiting at the inner door, peering in. He heard the first crack on the window and turned round to George, who was peering in from the outside door. Henry held his thumb up and George nodded but signaled for him to wait.

In the warehouse, after the third stone hit the windows, Professor Chillingworth looked up from his control panel.

"Mr. Sticks, what is that irritating noise? Find out please."

"May I remind you sir, that we are no longer employed by you. We completed our assignment and our transaction is complete. We only remain here until Miss Words arranges transportation. But as the noise may be said transportation, I will ask Mr. Stones to investigate"

Mr. Sticks signaled to Mr. Stones, who lumbered over to the front door, just as a pebble hit a crack in the window and smashed it, crashing through the pane and striking him in the face. The pebble hit Mr. Stones but didn't bounce off him, it just stuck to him and then was absorbed into his body. Mr. Stones burped briefly as if digesting something.

Outside, Flora whooped silently to herself as the stone smashed the window. Normally, breaking windows with pebbles would be naughty, but Flora decided that this was a rescue mission and there would be some collateral damage. Shortly after that she saw a big, hulking shadow moving behind the frosted glass of the window, and then she saw the door start to open.

She ducked back down behind the TO(I)LET sign, and tried to breathe quietly.

Meanwhile, Henry saw Mr. Stones leaving the building. Mr. Sticks and the scientist fellow were both watching the door, distracted. He looked back at George and signaled he was going in. George nodded and mouthed silently "*be careful.*"

Without any further delay, Henry crept into the main room and hid behind a chair. When he was sure that no one was watching him he dashed to the table. But Mr. March had been watching everything and spotted Henry sneaking towards the table. He smiled, a wolf-like grin.

Henry got to the table and hunched down for a moment, and once again checked the others were still distracted. They were and so he stood up, looked at the table top, and saw the set of keys. He grabbed them first time and dived back down. Then he turned and saw Mr. March signaling him. The cage was less than 10 feet away. Mr. March pointed and Henry saw that the scientist man had turned away from the front door, and was looking in their direction. If Henry moved from behind the table he would be seen.

"*Throw the keys*" mouthed Mr. March. Henry put his arms out questioningly, as he wasn't sure what Mr. March was saying. Mr. March mimed throwing, and then unlocking. Henry nodded excitedly, understanding. He put the keys in his left hand, his best hand, and threw them towards Mr. March. They flew through the air, spinning.

Mr. March poked his hand through the bars to try to catch them, and they were heading directly for him. But then they started to drop, not having enough momentum, and instead they went under Mr. March's outstretched palm, and hit a metal bar with a "***Clunk***". They bounced back just out of reach of Mr. Marchs hand as he tried to grab them through the bars.

Sticks and the scientist guy looked directly at them. Chillingworth saw Henry dart back behind the table.

"Mr. Sticks, It seems we have an intruder, be so good as to apprehend him for me."

Meanwhile, outside in front of the building, Mr. Stones slowly plodded towards the TO(I)LET sign. Flora hid, crouched down as low as she could, and bundled up into a ball by one of the wooden posts to make herself as small as possible. There was a street light in between the warehouse and the sign, and she could see that large square shadow of Stones starting to appear on the ground, over the sign, as he walked closer and closer. If he looked over the edge, surely Flora would be discovered.

She saw the top of his head over the sign, looming towards her. Soon he would see her.

Flora nearly panicked, but didn't. She thought very quickly. Looking down in her hand she saw she still had 3 pebbles left. Without thinking, as thinking would have outdone her, she cast them underhand as hard as she could, low and to the opposite side of the building. They hit the road, and clattered along. She saw the large head turn towards the new sounds, and stalk off towards the disturbance. It was now almost completely dark, and the stones had hit outside the coverage of the street light, in darkness.

Stones walked over, and Flora took her chance. She darted the opposite way, towards the access road to run to the back of the building. Stones turned and grunted in frustration, and saw the shadowy, fleeting figure of Flora darting down the side of the building. He turned and lumbered after her.

George was getting worried about Henry and so had crept into the staff room, and sneaked a peek around the door to the main warehouse. He saw Henry was crouched down behind the table, and Mr. March was reaching for something silver and shiny on the floor, something that was just out of reach.

LE

He heard voices.

"Professor that will require a new contract of employment. My associate and I do not work for beans or fresh air."

"Not now," shouted Chillingworth, frustrated "Get that child and I will pay you."

"But how much?" queried Mr. Sticks.

" A third as much again."

"A third as much again of the original payment, or as third as much again of the payment that had as third as much again added to it?" asked Mr. Sticks for clarification.

"Either, just get that boy."

"Very well, Professor. I just need a signature here", Mr. Sticks pulled the long vellum sheet of paper and a feather quill back out from his inside jacket pocket.

Chillingworth started to say something, but then grabbed the quill from Sticks, clearly annoyed and exasperated. He signed, but even more annoying was that his name took a long time to write.

He went to hand the quill back to Sticks.

"And here, here and here please. We have to cross the eyes and dot the teeth, don't we?"

Chillingworth sighed, and signed again and again and again.

"Now, bring me that child, Mr. Sticks," he demanded.

" And do not disturb me. We are approaching the end, and I need to concentrate on this stage."

He picked up a pair of headphones, placed them on his head, and plugged them into the control panel. He turned and looked at Sir Francis, who was so thin he now looked like a skull covered in tissue paper skin.

Sticks grinned, and once again stowed the parchment away in his jacket pocket. He started walking quickly towards the end of the warehouse, towards Henry.

George was about to act when he heard a noise behind him. He turned and saw a small dark figure dart through the outside door into the office.

"It worked, but a bit too well. He on his way," gasped Flora, half out of breath.

"Who?"

"The big grey man. Stones"

"What?" whispered George?

"He's following me from the front. He can't be more than a moment or three behind me."

Faced with an impossible choice, George made one.

"Flora, close the door, see if you can lock it, or barricade it. The Sticky fellow is after Henry. I must help him. That's the most immediate danger."

George dashed towards the front of the office and out of the door into the warehouse.

"OK" whispered Flora to no one, as George had already gone. She dashed to the back door and pulled it closed, just in time as then there was a "***Bang***" on the outside of the door. A huge fist shaped dent appeared in the top of the metal door. Fortuitously, the key was in the lock, and the door opened inwards. She managed to turn the key, and then she ran back and started pushing the table to the door to barricade it.

There was another almighty "***Bang***" and another fist sized dent appeared in the door. Flora figured the door would not hold him out for much longer. But how do you stop a man made of stone?, she asked herself.

Chapter Twenty Nine

Mr. Sticks was no more than 20 yards from Henry when George burst through the door. The door slammed against the wall and George jumped into the room, holding his hands in the air.

"Oy, Sticky fellow, over here!" he shouted.

Mr. Sticks stopped, almost equidistant from both Henry and George. He stared at George, but decided that Henry was the threat, as he could see the keys on the floor, and Mr. March had nearly got a fingertip to them.

Sticks turned to walk towards Henry.

"Oh, sticky fellow. Over here," tried George again "C'mon, you useless bag of rancid twigs and rotting branches."

Sticks stopped in his tracks. George knew he was onto something. If only he could anger him enough. He continued.

"C'mon you useless scarecrow, you suit stuffed with old foisty moss and stinky sludge. You are nothing but a walking bag of compost. I am going to take you home to my Mum, so she can spread you on her roses, the way she puts horse poo on them. At least then some good will come from your worthless existence."

Sticks turned, his face full of fury.

"You dare," he hissed.

"That's right, raggedy-no-man. The only brains in your head are from the mice who sleep in your rotting body."

Sticks was wild with rage.

"Do you know to whom you speak, boy? I was around in the shadows learning my trade when your species was still rubbing sticks together to make fire. I have seen a thousand of your type, and conquered them all. You have sealed your fate, boy," he almost spat at George.

George risked a glance at Henry, who was still behind the table. His eyes stared at Henry and then the keys, which Mr. March was still struggling to reach. Henry nodded, and waited for a moment.

"I'm not scared of a bundle of stinking putrid firewood. I'm not worried about a walking sack of compost. I'm not frightened by a malodorous mound of moss and muck."

Mr. Sticks actually screamed in rage, a high pitched wail, and charged at George, his hands in front of him like talons. George waited until Mr. Sticks was only a few feet away and turned and fled, running away from Henry and the cage, and towards Sir Francis.

Henry took the opportunity, and moved. He dashed across the short distance to the keys, and scooped them up and ran to the cage. He put the key in the lock and it turned with a click. The door was free, and Henry pulled it wide open and Mr. March exploded out of the cage, past Henry, and howled in anger.

Back in the staff room, Flora had piled all the furniture against the door, but with the regularity of a ticking clock, Mr. Stones beat his hands against it. Soon the top of the metal door was curved in like a bowl from the repeated blows. Then he struck again, and the inch thick steel fractured. A thin crack appeared. Another blow, and the crack got bigger. Soon it was a few inches long, and Flora saw in horror as the thick fingers of Mr. Stones started to push their way through the crack, and then close around it and started to pull. The steel started to peel away like the skin from a banana, but with a shriek of metal.

Flora could see the cold grey eyes of Mr. Stones staring through the gap. He stared straight at Flora, and continued rending the door open.

Flora knew she had only a matter of moments before Mr. Stones was in the room. But there was only her. How could she stop a creature made of stone, that was stronger than steel. What could possibly stop a walking mountain? A mobile statue? A moving cliff?

She stopped, and her eyes lit up, and a light bulb almost glowed above her head. What can destroy a cliff? What indeed!

She dashed towards the door into the main warehouse.

Chapter Thirty

George tried to run, but as fast as he was, Mr. Sticks was faster – and George was limited as he had to keep Sticks away from Henry. Sticks caught up with George and one of his hands reached out and closed on George's coat collar. George tried to dart behind a bench of equipment, but Mr. Sticks held him fast. He dropped down and slipped out of his coat and was free, but fell to the floor. Mr. Sticks cried out in frustration, an evil, thin sound.

George found himself on top of two black duffel bags. They were both unzipped. He reached his hand inside the first one, desperately looking for a weapon to defend himself with. His hand reached in, and disappeared to his shoulder. He almost fell into the bag, it was so unexpectedly deep. His hand grasped around inside, looking for something, anything.

Then Mr. Sticks was on him, and grabbed him by the shoulders.

"I will make you pay for those words, young Master Bannerworth. Yes I know who you are. I know the who, what, when, where and why of you all. And when I have made you pay, I will make your annoying little siblings pay as well," he sneered.

He pulled George to his feet, making George cry out in pain, but just as he did, George's hand closed on something cold and metal. He grasped it as he was hauled back up.

Across the room, Mr. March was in a fury. He raised his mouth to the ceiling and howled with rage. And then he started to change. But this time, he changed all at once.

His legs started to elongate and burst out of his brogue shoes. His toes turned into long claws, and his big toe was now halfway up his leg. His trousers split, as his muscles grew, his thighs becoming thrice their size. A short, muscular tail burst out from the base of his spine. His shoulders broadened and his back arched, splitting his jacket and shirt. His arm became as long as his legs, with the same long claws on paws where hands used to be. His face elongated all at once, his face turning into a muzzle, with deep set yellow slitted eyes, huge nostrils, and long ivory fangs. Fur grew all over his body, covering him with a thick dark pelt.

He shook free of the remnants of his clothes, and stood to his full height of 8 feet tall on his hind legs, and raised his snout and howled once more, but this was a howl of pure animal, feral rage.

"Blimey," cried Henry, Half terrified, half amazed. "Is that still you Mr. March?"

The giant wolf turned and stared at him, and moved his great snout to within an inch of Henry's face. The great wolf breathed out through his cavernous nostrils, and the air ruffled Henry's blonde hair. The breath was warm and stank of decay and death. Henry tried to back away, but he was against the side of the cage. Then Mr. March, or what was Mr. March, nuzzled Henry affectionately, and licked his face. Henry giggled.

Mr. March heard George's cry, and spun around and bounded across the room towards Mr. Sticks and George. Henry jumped to his feet and sprinted after him.

At the same time, Mr. Sticks raised his hand and put it around George's throat, and grinned horrifically.

"And now, young Master Bannerworth, you will regret your words to me," and started to squeeze.

George swung his arm up. He had happened to grab hold of the large crow bar that Mr. Stones had earlier used at Ratford House. He brought it up, and pushed the thin end into Sticks upper arm. It pierced right through. Mr. Sticks squealed in pain (if he could feel pain) and let go of George.

George pushed down on the crow bar, twisting it downwards. There were a lot of snapping sounds, and then he stumbled a couple of steps backwards as there was no longer any resistance. He looked down and saw that Mr. Sticks arm lay on the floor, its fingers still twitching.

Mr. Sticks screeched once more in rage, and went to lunge at George. But then he was thrown forward, as a huge furry figure leaped on his back. They tumbled forward, Sticks and Mr. March rolling in a ball. They came to a stop, and Mr. March was on top of Sticks, tearing with teeth and claws.

Soon, Sticks lay there like a pile of twigs. Both his arms and legs had been wrenched from his body, and the stuffing had been knocked out of his abdomen. Sticks looked around at his current state, and blinked several times, not believing what he was seeing.

Mr. March raised his snout and howled in triumph. Henry dashed over and hugged Mr. March, burying his head in the thick fur of the great wolf's body.

"What the......?" asked George, almost lost for words.

"It's Mr. March, he can turn into a wolf." explained Henry patiently, quite pleased that for once George didn't know everything.

"That's Mr. March?" said George, still not quite understanding.

"Yes of course, who else would it be?"

But as they talked, on the floor before them tendrils from Sticks body were starting to grow towards his arms and legs, as he tried to once more pull himself together.

Mr. March barked, and pointed with his nose at the figure on the floor.

"Henry, perhaps Mr. March would like to play fetch?" suggested George, looking down.

Henry smiled and picked up one of Mr. Sticks still wriggling arms and threw it. Mr. March watched it fly through the air, and took off after it, his short tail wagging merrily. He caught the arm in mid-air and brought it back to Henry, who next threw a leg.

Mr. Sticks lay there, helplessly, as Henry and Mr. March played their game. As soon as he was close to reforming one of his limbs, Henry would grab it and throw it across the room. Mr. March would chase it and bring it back, and put it down at Henry's feet, waggling his tail joyfully. He would sit there, his mouth open and his tongue flopped out happily, in a sort of wolfish grin, waiting for Henry to throw the next limb.

Mr. Sticks sighed to himself. He could regrow his limbs given time, but that would take hours or days.

"Blast it and darn them, they've turned me into a dog's toy. How embarrassing. My future employment prospects will no doubt suffer when word gets round about this," he muttered to himself.

George meanwhile, had not forgotten about Flora. He ran across the room to the door at the rear, and just as he got there Flora ran into the warehouse, and there was a huge crash from the staff room.

Mr. Stones had entered the building.

Chapter Thirty One

The door burst inwards, scattering the table, chairs and everything else that Flora had piled up behind it. A metal bin was hit with such force that it flew across the room, and through the now wide open door into the main warehouse. George was running towards the doorway and Flora, and the bin flew over Flora's head but hit George full in the chest. George was knocked backwards to the floor, stunned.

Mr. Stones kicked and pushed all the remaining debris out of the way and forced his way through the wrecked doorway. He strode across the small room, and arrived at the doorway into the main warehouse. He looked around, and saw George stunned on the floor; Flora running off to the left, scared. Across the room, Mr. Sticks was laying on the floor, in pieces, as Henry and Mr. March continued their fun game.

Mr. Stone's eyes started to glow red with fury. He was normally slow to anger, but seeing his partner of so many, many years reduced to a dog's toy infuriated him. He screamed, which sounded like a rock-fall, and strode across the room, closing the distance to Mr. Sticks.

George sat up, still dazed. His chest hurt like fire, and he had a bump on the back of his head from when he fell and hit the cold hard floor, but apart from that he seemed OK. He saw Stones closing on where Mr. March and Henry were happily playing, oblivious to the doom headed their way.

"Henry, watch out," he shouted, and Henry and Mr. March stopped and turned. Mr. March saw Stones walking across the floor. He howled and launched himself at Stones, and struck with claws and teeth.

But Stones was not a bag of twigs but had the power of boulders and rocks. Mr. March's claws sliced through the grey suit, but scratched harmlessly at the granite figure beneath. Stones just swatted him aside with a sweep of his huge arm. Mr. March went flying across the room, yelping, and crashed into a bench and fell to the floor, unconscious.

Henry shouted in anger, "Mr. March, you hurt Mr. March," and ran at Stones in a rage. His small hands beat at the column like legs, but all Henry ended up with was bruised knuckles.

Stones looked down on Henry, who gazed up in terror at the huge lumbering figure. A massive three fingered hand reached down to grab Henry. George looked on in horror, still sitting half upright on the floor as the huge fist closed in on the little boy.

"Noooooooooo," George screamed.

But then just as the fist was about to grab Henry, there was a huge jet of water. It came from the back of the room and hit Stones hand. First one finger, and then another, was worn down by the water, eroded in moments as the sea would erode a cliff over centuries. The fingers crumbled away, Stones help up his hand. Only the palm remained.

George and Henry looked on, amazed. Then they heard a whoop of triumph and delight from behind them. They turned and saw Flora, walking towards Mr. Stones. In her hands was the long, lance like nozzle of the pressure washer. On her back was strapped the heavy box of the unit, but she seemed to carry it without any problem. She advanced on Stones. Henry thought she looked like a Ghostbuster and cheered.

Flora pulled the trigger again, this time aiming at the broad chest of Stones. The lance of water cut past the torn remnants of Stones' suit, and hit the rock like chest. Stones looked down in horror as the jet of water started to hollow out his abdomen. Stone dust fell to the floor, mixing with the water, to create a sludge around Mr. Stones.

"PLEASE" he grumbled, imploring Flora to stop. She continued to approach relentlessly, keeping the water jet aimed at the huge figure.

Except the figure wasn't huge anymore. Flora continued to use the water lance the way a surgeon would use a scalpel. Soon, Stones had lost both of his arms, worn down to his shoulder. Then Flora targeted his legs. They were worn down in seconds into thin spindles, which eventually collapsed under the weight of Stones' body. He dropped to the floor with a thud. All that was left was the torso and head.

"PLEASE PLEASE STOP" he rumbled pleadingly.

But there was no pity in Flora's face. She kept the water concentrated on Stones' body, and slowly wore it away, until all that was left was Stones' head, standing on the floor, looking even more like an Easter Island statue. Stones blinked, and looked down at Sticks, who was staring up at him, still desperately trying to pull himself together, but the water jets had washed his limbs way across the room.

"DAMN" Mr. Stones griped "WHAT NOW?" he asked of Mr. Sticks

"To be honest, Mr. Stones, I really don't know," admitted Mr. Sticks, shrugging. Which was about all he could do without any limbs. "I'm very much afraid they have rendered us harmless. And armless. And legless."

Flora turned off the power washer but kept the lance in her hands just in case. George ran over to her and hugged her, saying,

"Clever girl. How did you know it would work?" he asked.

"Well, the only thing I could think of that could wear down a stone was the sea, and so it seemed like a good idea."

Meanwhile Henry ran over to Mr. March, who was still laying a bit stunned but had started to come around. But he had turned back to a human when he was unconscious, and when he opened his eyes he realised he was naked and went bright red in embarrassment.

Henry looked around and saw an old sheet, and grabbed it and threw it to Mr. March, who smiled gratefully and stood to his feet, a bit unsteadily, and wrapped it around him. He ruffled Henry's hair in thanks.

The two of them walked over to George and Flora who were still standing around the rather reduced forms of Sticks and Stones. Mr. March gathered up Sticks arms and legs, and threw them into the second duffle bag and zipped it up.

"Let's see you try to re-attach those," he grinned down at Sticks, who just groaned.

"Well, that all turned out rather well," he said to the kids

"We are not done yet," said George, "What about Sir Francis"

"Oh my, of course," said Mr. March. But before they had even moved there was a high-pitched laugh from the front of the warehouse. They turned as one, to see Professor Chillingworth standing there in triumph.

"YOU ARE TOO LATE, I HAVE PERFECTED MY SOLUTION," he yelled at the top of his voice, and held up the flask of green liquid in victory.

He took off his headphones and unplugged himself.

"Sorry, I was a bit loud then. However, if you would like to say goodbye to Sir Francis, then I suggest you do so now, as I am afraid he has given his all for science. As he will soon be dead," he smirked, then looked puzzled.

"Well, dead again really," he clarified, "but this time permanently"

Chapter Thirty Two

They all stood there in shock but then walked over to the bench. Chillingworth backed away, keeping his distance, but smiling happily.

"Say your farewells quickly, for soon I will be reborn to the night, and I doubtless will be a bit puckish," he grinned.

Then he raised the flask to his lips and drank deep.

Knowing there was nothing they could do to stop him, the kids decided to try to help Sir Francis. They and Mr. March gathered around the bench. Sir Francis was laying still on the bench, his eyes half open but almost unresponsive. His face was little more than a skull, and his visible arms and legs were thinner than the thinnest stick.

He was as pale as fresh snow and his recently acquired hair had fallen out. George looked at the control panel, and guessed which button would retract the needles. He pressed it, and was relieved when the small thin needles withdrew from Sir Francis' wrists and ankles. They unfastened the manacles and Mr. March lifted him off the gantry, cradling him as a grown up would a baby. He weighed next to nothing.

Sir Francis eyes flickered open and looked up at the hairy face "Maximus?" he asked in a voice as quiet as death.

Mr. March nodded.

"You have come back to me, you loyal wolf," Sir Francis whispered. "I am sorry. I did not expect to sleep for so long"

"There's no need, Sir Francis. I have stayed around. I knew you would wake up one day,", said Mr. March, with tears in his amber eyes. He sank to the floor, holding Sir Francis.

"George, there must be something we can do?" said Flora, clearly upset.

"I don't know," said George, "I really just don't know."

"George, have you got any glood?" queried Henry.

"Why, yes, in my backpack. Do you think it will work?"

"It's worth a try," shouted Flora, excitedly.

George took his pack off his back and rummaged around inside. He found the flask of glood. It was in a thermos flask and so it would still be nice and warm. He knelt down by Sir Francis and Mr. March held up his head. George unscrewed the top and put the flask to Sir Francis pale thin lips and gently tipped it.

Behind them, Professor Chillingworth was changing. His whole body seemed to throb as the green elixir took effect. His face became paler but with a green tint, his eyebrows became more arched. His face thinned, and his eyes started to glow with an unnatural green. His top front teeth elongated and became pointed. His hands lengthened and his nails grew. Power throbbed through his body, and so did a hunger - a dreadful hunger.

"BEHOLD," he shouted "I AM REBORN."

They all looked up at him, all except Mr. March who was trying to force the glood into Sir Francis' mouth. Professor Chillingworth was floating in the air, a few feet above the ground. His hair seemed to float behind him, green tinged. He grinned a terrible grin.

"I am no longer human. I will no longer age, or die, I will live forever. For I am now vampire."

"Vampyr, rhymes with seer," shouted all the kids in unison, from where they knelt around Sir Francis' still body.

"Be that as it may, I am now immortal and humans are my prey. I will make you regret that you ever entered my lair."

The children all laughed. Chillingworth paused, mid float.

"What are you laughing at?" he screamed.

"To be honest, if you don't mind me saying, it's not a very good choice for a lair," said Flora, defiantly.

"Yes," agreed Henry, "surely there must have been an old dungeon you could have found?"

"Or a hilltop fortress in the mountains?" suggested Flora.

"Or an underwater stronghold?" George chipped in.

The Professor shrieked in frustration,
"Look, do you know how hard it is to make a business out of vampyr hunting? And anyway, I think you should be more worried about other things."

"So who would like to have the honour of sharing my first drink with me?"

He started to float down towards the children, his talon like arms reaching out for them, a dreadful hunger in his eyes.

"Or more accurately, be my first drink?"

The children shrunk back, terrified.

Chapter Thirty Three

"No, you will not touch them, you scoundrel." cried out a weak voice.

Chillingworth looked down and saw Sir Francis staring up at him. He was half sat up, but still looked weak.

"Hah, I do not think you can stop me Sir Francis. You look like death warmed up," he smirked.

Sir Francis struggled to his feet.

"I would not be so sure, if I were you," he replied.

He grabbed the flask from Mr. March, and placed it to his lips and drained it in one long gulp. Immediately, he started to improve. His skull like face filled out. His legs and arms thickened and his eyes glowed green. He floated up into the air, facing Chillingworth.

Mr. March then stood to his feet, and once more turned into the great wolf form. The kids then stood up and they all faced the mad Professor. George picked up the crow bar, and Flora the pressure washer and aimed it at Chillingworth. Henry grabbed a broken wooden chair leg that was lying around. It looked like a pretty good stake.

"It seems you are outnumbered and outmatched, Professor," said Sir Francis, his strength now returned to his voice "Do you think you can best us all?"

Sir Francis drew himself up to his full height and seemed to radiate power. A green glow surrounded him.

Panic crossed Chillingworth's face, he was a being just come into his power and he didn't know if he could beat them all.

"You have bested me this day, Varney, but mark my words. I am your nemesis. I will be back. I will track each of you down and defeat you. Nowhere on this earth will you be free of me. But now I must fly and feast on others."

He laughed manically, and floated up to the ceiling and then with a puff of green smoke he turned into a bat.

Except he didn't.

Instead the green squirrel that appeared in the bat's place looked slightly startled as it suddenly found itself in mid-air. It looked around as if just realising it was several metres off the ground. It frantically flapped its wings to no avail. With no momentum, Chillingworth plummeted to the floor. He hit hard, and lay there stunned.

"The cage," shouted George.

Flora picked up the dazed green squirrel by its bushy tail, and ran to the silver cage. She threw the Professor inside and Henry slammed the door, and locked it. He threw the keys to George who put them in his pocket.

"Phew, that is quite a relief," said Sir Francis, who was still floating in the air towards where they were clustered around the cage. He started to drop back down to earth, but juddered from side to side as he did so. When he landed, he staggered to the left, and George had to catch him.

"Are you OK, Sir Francis," he asked, deeply concerned.

"I will be my boy, I will be. Thanks to you three. But it took all my strength to fly up like that"

"So it was a bluff?" questioned Flora.

"Well, on my part. I have little strength and used most of it to challenge him. But I knew that even if I failed, you three and Maximus would not", he smiled, horrifically.

"But what of Chillingworth? Won't he just change to smoke, or gloop, and escape the cage?" asked George, looking at the green squirrel that was hanging by its claws from the side of the cage.

"He can't" said Mr. March, who was once again human and wrapped in a blanket, shivering. "The cage is made of silver. Silver has power over both vampyrs and lycan"

"Lychen?" asked Henry.

"No lycan, rhymes with van," said Sir Francis weakly, unable to help himself.

"Yes lycan, or were-creatures like me. Neither vampyrs nor lycan can change form when imprisoned in silver. That's why I couldn't change and break out of the cage earlier," explained Mr. March.

"So that means he's stuck like that-" started George.

"-And I get a pet squirrel" shouted Flora, delighted. "I will make him a perch to sit on. And a wheel to run in. And I will get him some little toys he can play with. And a water bottle I can fill with liquidised spinach for him to drink…"

They all looked at her amazed and then burst out laughing.

In the cage, the green squirrel looked up in horror at Flora.

Chapter Thirty Four

It all took a bit of time to sort everything out. First of all they had to decide what to do with Mr. Sticks and Mr. Stones, but Mr. March had a solution.

"Have any of you got your phone?" he asked the kids.

Immediately 3 smartphones were thrust into his face. He grabbed one and made a call.

"Mr. H" he began "It's Mr. M. What? Oh yes, me using a phone. It is a first. But I must apologise for the hour. What? It's only half past seven? Really it seems much later. But I have a favour to ask. No, two favours in fact."

Mr. March explained down the phone and then about 10 minutes later hung up.

"My good friend Mr. H is going to help us. First with these two miscreants," he said, pointing down at the glum looking faces of Sticks and Stones.

"We should be expecting contact imminently," he said.

Just as he finished there was a flash of light came down through the roof, forming a circle on the floor. The light was so bright they had to avert their eyes.

Then the light dimmed, and standing in the circle was a young woman. She was tall, and slender with long white hair, but a smooth ageless face. She was wearing a white double breasted leather jacket and a white pencil skirt.

"I understand I am here to see a Mr. Marchdale?" she asked, in a voice like honey, *"My name is Miss Words, and I understand you have two of my associates?"*

Mr. March walked forward and pointed to Stones head and Sticks head and torso on the floor.

"Oh, my, they have been in the wars haven't they? You did this to them?" she asked of Mr. March.

"I didn't. They did," he replied, pointing at the three kids. Miss Words looked at the Bannerworths, looking first slightly shocked and then respectful.

"Impressive. But we must talk terms," Miss Words continued. She seemed charming in every way.

"Yes, first of all, they must swear that they will never seek to harm any of us, or our friends and family again" said Mr. March.

"Agreed. Anything else?"

"That they pay reparations to Sir Francis for their treatment of him"

"Oh for Petes' sake," they heard Sticks grumble from the floor "I knew it would be the money. Blast it Mr. Stones. They want our money"

"*Agreed*", Miss Words gestured and a sack of coins appeared on the ground, next to Sir Francis. The coins were gold, round, large and rough, with a skull on one side.

"Can we go now?" asked Miss Words.

"Not so fast," said Mr. March, pulling a vellum piece of paper and a quill pen from Stick's pocket "They must sign first."

"Sign?" protested Sticks "You may have failed to notice, you big ball of fur, that I have no arms."

"George, if you would be so kind," said Mr. March, pointing at the duffel bags.

George almost burst out laughing, but went to the duffel bags and rummaged around. He found one of Sticks arms, or rather it found him and grabbed his wrist. He pulled it out of the bag, and held it by the elbow, and pulled so that the hand let go of him. Mr. March put the quill in the arms' hand and told Sticks,

"Sign."

"But I'm left handed. That's clearly my right hand, you dullard." protested Sticks.

"Just do it."

The hand George was holding scribbled on the vellum paper. "And here, and here, and here," said George, pointing.

"You do realise it is quite hard to see from here," said Sticks mournfully from his place on the floor.

"Sign here, here and here," George insisted "We have to stop the lies and halt the tears"

Sticks grumbled, but signed here, here and here.

"What about him?" asked Flora, pointed at the disembodied head of Stones.

"Ah good point, but how do we make him sign?" asked George "As his arms seem to have turned to sand."

In the end they put the feather quill in Stones wide mouth, feather first, and all he could do was make a cross in black ink.

"And here, here and here," insisted George.

Stones growled, a sound like an avalanche rumbling down from the mountains, but he made his mark three more times.

George rolled up the vellum parchment and put it inside his backpack.

"Right, all appears to be in order," said Miss Words pleasantly.

"It's been a pleasure doing business with you," she added, sweetly *"Although maybe not for those two,"* she laughed, staring down at her colleagues.

She walked over and stood between Stones head and Sticks body, taking the two duffel bags with her. She raised her hand to the sky, and another flash of light. When it dimmed, there was no sign of Sticks, Stones or Miss Words.

"But what about him?" asked George, pointing at the small green squirrel in the rather large cage.

"Everything is in order, George. Wait and see," replied Mr. March.

Shortly after, a man turned up in an ancient looking van that said "CHAR AND ANTI AGE BOO HOP" on its side in peeling gold letters. Mr. March and this new, rather bookish, looking man, loaded the silver cage into the back of the van.

"What are we doing with him?" asked George of Sir Francis, pointing at the small furry form of Chillingworth.

"Well, as I made him of sorts, he is now my son, again of sorts. And so I have a responsibility to look after him. We will take him back to Ratford House, and we can place him and his gilded cage in a nice draughty room."

"Can I visit and feed him?" asked Flora excitedly.

"Of course, my dear. I am sure the Professor would want nothing less."

In the cage, the green squirrel groaned to himself. He feared he was in for a very long and boring few years (or centuries).

Epilogue

Elsewhere........

Imagine a castle. It's an old Castle, set on a high craggy peak in the Carpathian Mountains. It has thin and tall spires and turrets, and in the walls have tall and thin windows. In the middle is a large oak front door, bound with iron, which rarely opens. The paint is peeling from the door and the window frames. The mortar of the huge stones of the building are crumbling and the whole castle smells of damp and decay.

There is only one road to The Castle. It's only a carriage wide, and it twists and turns its way from the foot of the mountain to the door; and turns and twists from the door back down - if you ever manage to escape! The road climbs up to The Castle with a steep fall on either side.

It's never sunny around The Castle. The skies are always dark and cloudy, even in the height of summer. Fork lightning constantly crashes across the sky, and flicks the tops of the mountains, briefly lighting up the dark castle.

There's rarely any light at the windows, except in the top of the tallest spire that reaches to the sky like a dark finger.

No one comes and goes to The Castle.
No carriages ever drive up the twisting road.
No visitors never approach the door, and no one enters by the door.
Wolves can be heard baying in the mountains, and large bats flutter around the turrets of The Castle, sometimes entering by a window, sometimes leaving.

This is the seat of all vampyr power in the world. It's the home of the The Vampyr Council, or The Council of Vampyrs.

In the tallest spire, in the topmost level, is a room. It's a large, dark room, with a massive open fireplace, that is always lit. As vampyrs don't feel the cold, then the only logical reason for the fire is that it looks dramatic.

There are iron sconces in the walls, holding flickering candles that, with the fire, help light the room. Although if you look closer you will actually see that they are not real candles, but those fake candle light bulbs that flicker away. Sometime ago, after they ran out of candles and sat in the dark for five years, the Council had finally got around to getting electricity installed.

In the centre of the room is a large table, made of a single piece of smooth white marble, and around it are thirteen white marble chairs. You would expect that the table would have been made from basalt or obsidian, or some other dark stone as it would look more dramatic.

One chair is taller than the others, and at the end of the table, and the other twelve are arranged six on each side. The taller chair is the chair of the President of the Council.

The current head of the council is Strigoi, an ancient vampyr of unbelievable power. He is tall and spindly, with a huge, bald head, thin face and high cheekbones. His ears are long and pointed, but his left one is bent.

He sits in his throne-like chair, trying not to squirm in discomfort. He curses whoever had voted to change the chairs from the old comfy leather ones, to these marble monstrosities. Unnaturally thin, his backside aches from having to sit on the hard stone chairs.

He briefly considers calling for a vote to buy some new chairs, but decides against it for three reasons:
1. He must not appear weak in front of his brethren;
2. A vote to change the chairs would require endless debate and endless rounds of voting, and finally;
3. Even if he did get the vote to change the chairs, it's so hard to get IKEA to deliver.

He squirms, regretting not sneaking a velvet cushion into the chamber. Vampyrs can feel pain and discomfort, and right now he shifts from left to right as parts of his bum go numb.

He is dressed in a double breasted black leather jacket with a huge high collar. The effect was supposed to be majestic and menacing, and it may have been in the 1950's, but today it made him look a bit like a cheap B movie villain. It's also really uncomfortable, as the leather is thick and new, and it makes it hard from him to bend his arms to have a drink.

On the marble table in front of him is a tall slim bottle of red wine, or at least it appears to be red wine. Next to it is a tall crystal glass, half full of the red liquid, which is a bit too thick and gloopy to be wine. He picks up the glass, and tries to have a sip, but he looks distinctly un-presidential as he cannot bend his arm enough and has to crane his long neck towards the glass.

He thinks about calling for a long plastic straw, but decides against it. Firstly it would look ridiculous, and also the Council had recently committed towards becoming more carbon neutral and so had banned the use of non-recyclable plastic in The Castle.

He manages to get a sip and it's worth it. It's an extremely good vintage. It's a Dumas from December 1870, full bodied, with a hint of spice. He savors the red liquid as it slides down his dry throat. As he ingests it, he has images of three, no, four men in wide plumed hats, tabards and long sabers, fighting other men with crosses on their tabards.

He shakes his head to free the images. This often happens with bottled vintages.

All the other chairs were occupied by the other members of the Council.

"So, my brethren" starts Strigoi, in a hollow, booming voice that echoes off the high ceilings of the vaulted room. He quite likes the effect and he had made sure his chair was placed in the part of the chamber that had the best acoustics.

"We have news from afar. Apparently, one of our subjects has risen from a deep slumber in Angleland. He was sought out and captured by some mortal, with the aide of some ancient power, as the mortal tried to find the secret of our immortality."

There was a gasp of shock from the members of the Council. Strigoi smiled thinly, enjoying knowing something the Council did not.

"It appears that the subject was rescued, with the aid of a lycan, but mainly by three mortal children. And worse, our subject did not even try to drink the children, and appears to have formed some sort of "friendship", I think that's the word, with them."

More gasps and sharp intakes of non-breath. Strigoi looks increasingly happy. It's always good to be the first with the gossip.

"We need to act. And act now. This cannot be allowed to continue – for one of our kind to become close to a mortal, let alone three mortals. I propose we send a Vampyr Hunter to track him down."

"A Vampry Hunter? We align with our enemies?" asks Carmilla, a relatively new member of the Council, as she was only 400 years old.

"The Hunter will not know that they are working for us, but this outrage cannot be allowed to continue. I took the chance to work through a mortal agent to contact one of the most feared of these Hunters, and here I have his response."

He picks up a rolled parchment, sealed with a blood red blob of wax. Vampyrs still haven't got the idea of emails or instant messaging, and there wasn't even Wi-Fi in the castle, and the 4G signal is terrible this high up in the mountains.

He slit the wax seal with a long sharp fingernail and unrolled it.

"Ah here we are, I enquired, through a third party, if we could retain the services of Vampyr Hunter D."

There was muttering all around. D was legend, a Vampyr Hunter of unsurpassed skill and ability, who had killed many of vampyr kind. He also looked pretty cool, with his long dark hair, wide hat and cape.

Strigoi reads the parchment, his lips moving as he did so, "Blah blah blah blah, this mortal really goes on. Oh here we are, this is the bit. "Our enquires have been unsuccessful as the agent required is currently occupied in the Far East.", oh, it looks like he is busy, that is a shame."

There are groans from the floor. Most of the Council sound upset.

Strigoi reads on "Blah blah blah blah again. Get to the point, man. Ah, but apparently he has recommended one of his associates. We are able to retain the services of.......................
Strigoi deliberately stops, partly to savor the moment, but mainly as he hasn't heard of this other hunter either – and so he's a bit shocked.

Vampry Hunter B."

There's muttering around the chamber:
"Who?"

"Never heard of him."
"No, me neither."
"That's a shame, D looks great in a cape."
"Has this B killed anyone you know?"
"And that hat, so cool."
"No not that I've heard."
"D killed my maker you know? Very professional work. Sliced his head clean off."
"Well isn't there anyone else available. Is Van Helsing still working?"
"And he's got amazing hair. So long and flowing. I wonder if he uses conditioner?"
"I heard he had retired."
"And that long sword."
"What about Blade?"
"And the pale skin. Almost as pale as a vampyr."
"I don't think he's real. Isn't he just a comic character?"

"My brethren, please calm yourselves. Arrangements have been made but I now open the floor so we can debate before we vote and, hopefully, proceed."

Inwardly, Strigoi sighed. Debates always went on forever, sometimes almost literally, and then there would no doubt be hundreds of rounds of voting. It was going to be a long night, or more likely, a long few months.

TO BE CONTINUED IN:

VARNEY THE VAMPYR 2: VAMPYR HUNTER B

Escape from The Archives

A Bonus Adventure starring Mr. March

Mr. March has got lost in The Archives. Again! In this interactive adventure, can you guide Mr. March through The Archives, so that he can get back home for tea.

You choose which route Mr. March takes - but beware! There may be anything around any corner.

A piece of paper, a pencil and an eraser may be useful as The Archives are easy to get lost in!

Each section you read, you will be given a choice. For example, if you want to turn left, go to Section 15. If you want to turn right, go to Section 31. So if you choose to turn right, then you turn to the paragraph that starts with the number 31.

Good luck - you may need it!

Oh and by the way, some of the things you may learn in The Archives may be true, mostly true, partly true (but mostly false) or downright balderdash!

1

"Mr. H" shouted Mr. March, increasingly frustrated.

Following the close call with Professor Chillingworth and Sticks and Stones, Mr. March had returned a few days later to "CHAR AND ANTI AGE BOO HOP", or Mr. Holland's book shop. He had been worried in case anyone else decided to come after Sir Francis, and especially the children. So he had decided to speak to his old friend Mr. H.

As usual, this meant that they had to go into The Archives to do some serious research. Mr. March didn't like The Archives much. Being a lycan, he normally had an incredible sense of where he was, and he never, never, ever, got lost – as long as his feet were in touch with the ground. He could sense the electromagnetic pull of the poles, so he always knew which way was north, and when he was on a path he could always find his way back. Except in The Archives.

He also had an unbelievable sense of smell and hearing, and could normally sniff out if someone had walked down a route, even 3 days later, or hear a pin drop half a mile away. Except in The Archives.

It was almost as if The Archives did not exist on earth. It was almost as if they were in another dimension, or another plane of existence. He kept thinking to ask Mr. H, but every time he did, something came up to make him conveniently (or inconveniently) forget.

They had only been in The Archives about half an hour when Mr. H had decided that he needed to go any get something. He had told Mr. March to wait where he was, as he would only be 5 minutes. That was 2 hours ago. Or seemed to be. Time was also tricky in The Archives. It was entirely possible that Mr. H had forgotten about him, as Mr. H often forgot anything that wasn't written down. Or, had something happened to him?

Either way, Mr. March decided that he must try to find Mr. H, or the way out, or hopefully both!

He is in a cul-de-sac of bookshelves - of which there are many in The Archives. A cul-de-sac is just a fancy way of saying a dead end. He walks out, and sees that the bookcases and shelves spread out in front of him, and to the left and the right.

Do you want Mr. March to?

Go left, turn to **5**

Go straight on, turn to **39**

Go right, turn to **48**

2

As Mr. March picks up the book he hears a "*click*" from behind the bookshelf. Then the whole shelf swings back on a hidden hinge and into another corridor. Mr. March walks through it, and the shelf swings back into place with a "*clunk*"

Turn to **28**

3

This corridor is small and dark, dank and damp, musty and foisty. The bookshelves on either side seem to be made out of living trees, and they seem to loom over Mr. March as he walks along the corridor.

On these tree-like shelves, as well as books, there are mushrooms and toadstools growing from the trees. Various plants grow from the shelves and in parts the shelves are covered in mold.

To Mr. March's senses, then it was all quite overwhelming. The corridor, or more like a passageway through a deep dark woods, narrowed and closed in around Mr. March's lanky form.

Soon, he could not get any further and resolved to turn around. As he is about to turn he sees in front of him a large toadstool, with a red cap covered in white dots.

If you want Mr. March to take the toadstool, turn to **8**
If you want him to ignore it, turn to **45**

4

As soon as Mr. March picks up the book, a puff of smoke engulfs him, and he feels like he is moving through space. He reappears in another corridor.

Turn to **26**

5

Mr. March walks down the left corridor, struggling at times to squeeze through the piles of books that litter the floor. The corridor seems to twist and turn and nothing seems straight, so that when he looks back, he cannot see more than 10 feet behind him.

Soon he arrives at another junction, if it can be called that and has the choice of three different routes.

To go left with Mr. March, turn to **38**; to go straight on, turn to **35**, to go right, turn to **44**

6

The corridors of The Archive seem endless. But eventually Mr. March arrives at yet another crossroads. Mr. March grumbles to himself "I can understand why they are called crossroads, as every time I get to another one, I get really angry"

For Mr. March to go right, turn to **27**
To go, left turn to **16**
To go straight on, turn to **21**

7

Another corridor lined with bookcases and books. Another one! Mr. March shakes his head in frustration and walks along the annoyingly similar corridor, until he arrives at a turning to the left, or another corridor straight ahead.

Do you want Mr. March to?
Go left, down the long corridor, turn to **30**
Go down the corridor ahead, turn to **25**

8

Mr. March plucks up the large red toadstool. He is starving, as he loves his food and normally eats every two hours.
He looks at the toadstool longingly.

If you decide to let Mr. March eat it, turn to **40**
Otherwise turn to **45**

9

Mr. March pours some more tea from the silver tea pot, and tops the cup up with a spot of milk. He settles back in one of the large armchairs and opens the book and starts to read.

"There is not one Archives in this world, but nine, one on each continent. Plus a spare one in the Arctic."

"Odd" thought Mr. March "I was sure there were only seven continents", but he carried on reading.

"Each Archive has its own responsibility to collect all that is written on their theme. Each has a custodian whose functions are to gather, catalogue and safely store every book every written (and a few that haven't been written) in their area of responsibility.

The European Archive focuses on books to do with the earth, and the beings that live on it, natural and supernatural. The Asian Archive focuses on the arts. The Antipodean Archive focuses on the history of individuals and cultures who live on the earth (and elsewhere). The North American Archive collects all works of fiction"

"I bet Sir Francis would love that one the most" thought Mr. March, "especially for all the Jackie Collins books". He chuckled to himself and carried on reading.

"The Arctic Archive gathers all works on science, and the Antarctic Archives stores all works on magic. The African Archive focuses on culture, and the South American Archive on the solar systems and space and beyond. Finally, the Atlantian Archives collects all works on other dimensions and realities.

Despite each Archive focusing on a theme, there are overlaps. So a novel about, for example, a ghost would be collected by both the European Archive (supernatural) and North American (fiction).

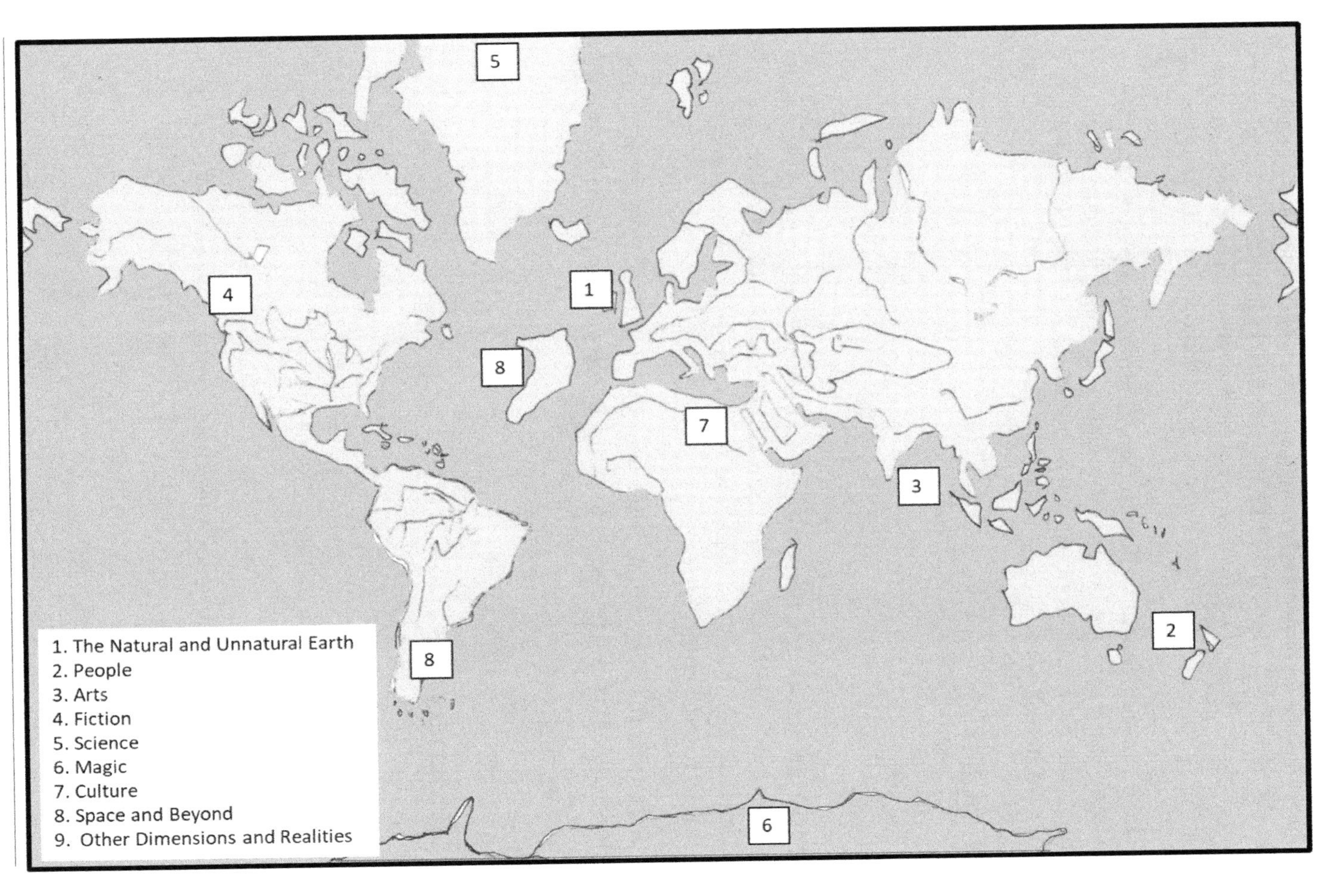
5
4
1
8
7
3
2
8
6
1. The Natural and Unnatural Earth
2. People
3. Arts
4. Fiction
5. Science
6. Magic
7. Culture
8. Space and Beyond
9. Other Dimensions and Realities

Each Archive is connected by a network, allowing custodians to borrow books from each other – a bit like an inter-library loan. Each Archive also is larger than you can possibly imagine, and exists in a place that is not quite of this earth. To find out more, please contact the Atlantian Archives"

The book then started off with dates, names and places, and Mr. March started to get bored. He finished off his third cup of tea, put the book back and stood up. He walked back to the door and left the Archive Room.

Turn to **12**

10

Mr. March pulls the book called "***Character***" out of the box. As he does so, the bookcase to his right slides to one side to reveal a doorway. Mr. March shrugs and walks through it. The bookcase slams closed behind him.

He finds himself in a place that seems very familiar. He is in a cul-de-sac of shelves. He curses to himself. Do you want Mr. March to?

Go left, turn to **5**

Go straight on, turn to **39**

Go right, turn to **48**

11

There's a short twisting corridor that eventually comes out into a longer corridor.

Turn to **30**

12

Mr. March is at a T-junction. He can either turn left of right.
To go left, turn to **34**
To go right, turn to **6**

13

Mr. March picks up a book and turns to the title page. It simply says "***Argent***", but it has no author underneath it. He frowns, as the name sounds familiar, and so it should.

He starts to read the prologue

"Argent comes from the Latin term Argentum, which means white metal. Argent is more commonly known as silver, and mirrors the colour of the moon."

"Aha" thought Mr. March, "that's why I know the name"

Mr. March didn't have the best memory for facts, which is one of the reasons why he liked Mr. H so much.

He flicks through the book and stops randomly at chapter 13, entitled "*The moon and the wolf, and others*" and starts to read

"It is well known in paranormal circles that silver has power over various supernatural creatures. As it is like the moon, that triggers the change of Lycan into their animal form, it holds the power to stop that change.

A lycan in human form, if held by silver, cannot transform into their were-form. Similarly, a lycan in were-form cannot change to human if held by silver.

Silver seems to trap the rays of the moon that trigger the change, and stop the moons power reaching the lycan, so they cannot transform. For this reason, many lycan wait out the full moon cycle in rooms or cages made of silver.

In addition, silver also has power over vampyrs. It cannot harm them, as the moon symbolises the night, when vampyrs are at their strongest. However it can stop them from changing into their other forms, such as a bat, mist or a mischief of rats. There are many theories for why this effects vampyrs. They include..."

Mr. March stopped reading. He didn't like science much, as he was a creature of instinct and action, not thought and learning, and so he was quickly bored. But then he laughed to himself,

"Bats, rats or mist no more! Well at least not for Sir Francis, or that good-for-nothing professor. Green squirrels, sludge and a bury of rabbits now!"

Still chuckling, he closed the book and dropped it back on the table. He turned and walks out of the "***Metals and Ores***" section. He walks to the end of the section and turns right onto the main corridor.

Turn to **37**

14

The bookcase clunks shut and locks. There is only one way to go, and so Mr. March plods on. He feels like he is underground, as there are no books or bookcases lining the walls. This time there are pipes above him, and he can feel the heat coming from them, and the hiss of gas. It reminds him of the basement of a large hospital still run on steam.

He is pleased when the corridor starts to open up. Were-wolves are not too keen on being underground, unless it's a wolfs den. They prefer to be able to see the sky, and feel the earth under their feet. Sadly Mr. March can do neither here, but he is still relieved to be in an almost normal section of The Archives.

Ahead of him is a panel in the wall. He pushs it, and it falls open into another corridor. He walks through, and the panel slams closed, and seamlessly blends in with the walls.

He is now faced with another choice. He is getting a bit sick of choices!

He can now either go through a door behind him, turn to **22**
Or go up the corridor to his left, turn to **53**

15

Mr. March pulls the book called "***Conflict***" out of the box. As he does so, the bookcase ahead of him slides to one side to reveal a doorway. Mr. March walks through it.

Turn to **14**

16

Mr. March plods down another seemingly identical book-lined corridor, and finally finds himself with another choice of directions. Do you want Mr. March to?

Go left, turn to **33**
Carry straight on, turn to **55**

17

Walking back to the main corridor, Mr. March doesn't want to go back the way he came, as he can recognise that way (for now) and so he has no alternative to turn right.

Turn to **37**

18

Mr. March leaves the *"Ancient History"* section, and retraces his steps back to the junction. You can either get Mr. March to:

Go left with Mr. March, turn to **35**;
Go straight on, turn to **44**

19

Another crossroads. Mr. March, whose personality is normally like that of an excited puppy, growls to himself in frustration? His bad mood is compounded by the fact that he never, ever, ever normally gets lost. He really must ask Mr. H why he keeps getting lost in The Archives – if he ever finds him!

However the choices for Mr. March are:
Go left, turn to **24**
Head straight on, turn to **18**
Go right, turn to **34**

20

Mr. March once again finds himself at a crossroads.

"Got more crossroads than Milton Keynes has roundabouts" he thinks to himself.

Should he:
Go right, turn to **21**
Head straight on, turn to **16**
Go left, turn to **34**

21

As the endless corridor carries on, eventually Mr. March finds a turn to the left. Mr. March can either:
Turn left, turn to **32**
Go straight on to **41**

22

Mr. March opens the door and found a small room. Unlike any of the others rooms he has seen, there were few books, but instead metal benches, covered in various bits of recording equipment, photos, transcripts and surveillance notes. Mr. March recognises its all of the Bannerworths and Sir Francis. He then realises that Mr. H must have got hold of all of Sticks and Stones surveillance notes.

He goes over to one of the reel to reel tape recorders (ask your parents!). There is a strange adaption on the microphone attached to it. He clicks the play switch and listens:

"Speaking of books, is Dracula real?"

(Mr. March straight away recognises the voice of George.
This must be a recording of the kids. Then he heard a strange voice)

"Hmmm, yes he is, unfortunately"

("Interesting", Mr. March thought to himself, "somehow they have found a way to record a vampyr". The recording continues)

George: "So the book was true?"

"Well not exactly. There was a time when some vampyrs thought it was a good idea to tell our stories to up and coming authors. It's hard to get a job when you look like we do"

"Maybe you could be in the movies, playing a vampyr. Save a fortune in special effects and make up"

"Well, one of us tried that. A friend of mine called Schreck. He was in a film in 1922. He hated it though. Being around all those people and not being able to have a drink when you wanted one. It would be like putting a dog in charge of a butchers store and expecting it not to eat all of the sausages.

So when the production was onto its 9th cameraman and 7th leading lady, as the others had disappeared, then things got a bit awkward and hard to explain away, and Schreck decided to leave. And all the bright lights-"

Henry: "But light doesn't kill you"

("Ah, trust Henry to ask a direct question", thought Mr. March)

"Yes but it makes us feel a bit dizzy, so we try and avoid it. That's why we never have a tan and you don't find many vampyrs living in Benidorm. And as Max had to leave the filming due to his diet habits, they had to make up the ending. Max had disappeared-"

"Into a puff of smoke?"

"No, he just jumped on the number 53 bus from Wismar. But as I was saying, in the film he dies from exposure to sunlight. The film had run out of money and couldn't find anyone else who looked like old Schreck. Wonder where he is now. Not heard from him since the Spanish Flu hit in 1917. We had a great year"

George: "A great year? During a plague?"

"Vampyrs love a good plague or a good war"

"That's horrible! Why"

"Well the problem is these days is that if you want to drink a person, then people tend to notice if they've gone missing, or if they turn up dead mysteriously"

"So how does a war help?"

"Well during World War 2, you could drink someone and then just lie them on the ground near a bomb site and put some rubble on top of them. People just assumed that a house fell on them or something"

"What about a plague"

"Well during a plague, the main thing is to get rid of dead bodies so the living don't get infected– and so no one really takes much notice of how they died and just assumes it's the plague. They just tend to cart them off and dump them in a big hole."

But, as I was saying, it's hard to make ends meet when you are a vampyr. And old houses have terrible overheads and cost a fortune to stop them falling into wreck and ruin."

(Mr. March snorts with laughter. To say that Ratford House was in wreck and ruin was being kind to the house. It was a bit of a tip)

"So a bit of quick money was always nice – and Dracula tended to twist the truth a bit to make his story a more romantic, exciting and gory"

"So the book Dracula is made up?"

(Henry again. Mr. March would guess that Henry wouldn't be interested in the book anyway as it did not contain any trucks or diggers. Henry only liked books with trucks or diggers in them.)

"Not made up exactly, more exaggerated"

George: "Such as?"

"Well, he was never a Count to start off with, and not known as Vlad the Impaler. When he became a vampyr he was just called Bradley Naylor, and he worked in the fields in Lincolnshire. His real nickname was Brad the Baler, as he used to bail up all the hay for the horses."

He only got turned accidentally when he uncovered an old vampyr sleeping in a sideboard in a barn. It was still daytime and the poor old guy was a bit confused, and turned him accidentally as he was half asleep"

"So, he's not from Transylvania?"

"No, not originally. After he sold his story to that hack of an author–"

"Bram Stoker"

"Yes that the one. After he sold his story, then he used the money to buy a big old castle in Transylvania. He changed his name to Vlad Dracula, managed to bribe a local official into being named a Count.

Then he started talking in that terrible accent. "I Vant to Dwink your Bluud""

"How did he used to say it?"

"Ah wan' ter drink yer blud" replied Sir Francis.

Henry: "That's not very scary"

("Typical Henry", thought Mr. March, "not much rattles him")

"No I suppose not. Then it was the capes, the horse drawn carriages, the suits. Calling himself Vlad the Impaler. Prior to that he just lived in the attic of a terrace house in Skegness and wore overalls"

"So is he not very old?"

"Pah, no! Not for a vampyr. He had only been a vampyr for 10 years when he told everything to Stoker. He must only be 140 at the most"

George: "134, Dracula was published in 1897"

(Mr. March wondered if George knew this, as he knew a lot of facts, but he guessed that he probably had looked it up on Wikipedia on his phone and wanted to look like he knew it off the top of his head)

"Well, even worse. He is but a child!"

"So how come no one has written a book about you? As you are so much older"

"They did"

"Really? What's it called?"

"Varney the Vampyr: The Feast of Blood. It was quite the hit at the time. It was serialised weekly in a magazine and was very popular. Quite the page turner it was. And published 50 years before Dracula. But who gets all the fame and glory? And all the films?"

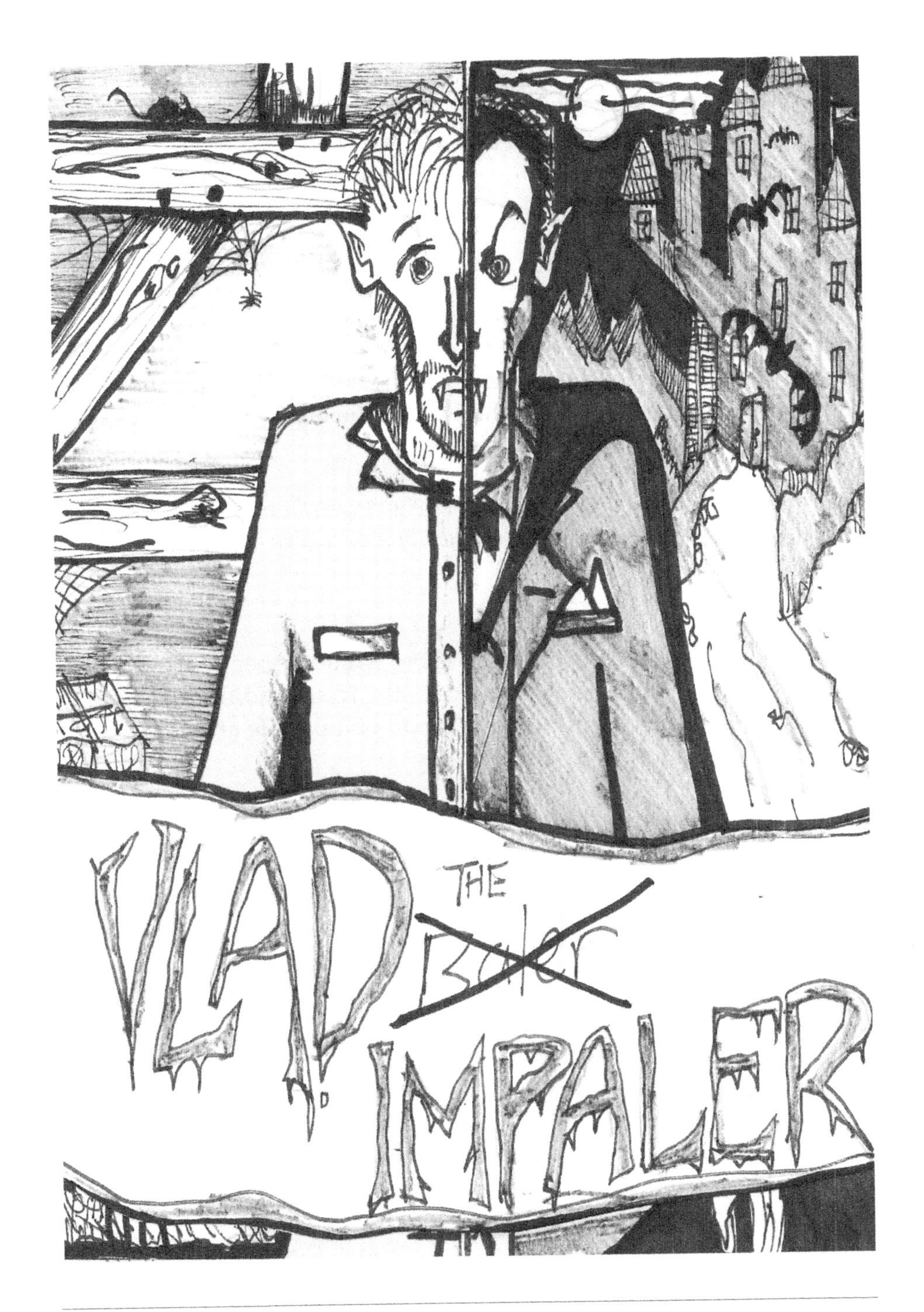
VLAD
THE
IMPALER

(Mr. March thought that Sir Francis sounded a bit grumpy on the tape. Sir Francis took a deep breath in to calm himself, which was a wasted effort as vampyrs don't breathe)

"But isn't it a good idea that people don't know you exist?"

"Well, there is that"

(Mr. March absently wondered why Flora was so quiet. Then he realised that this must have taken place when she had to go back to the house to warm up the glood - George had told him all about it. This must all have been put in here as all the talk was slowing down the plot of the story. But back to books)

Henry: "And maybe one day someone else will write a new book about you, then you can be famous and have all the flame and gory"

George: "Fame and Glory, Henry"

Mr. March stopped the tape, as he knew what happened from hereon in. Shrugging, Mr. March scans the room and finds little of interest. He does have the attention span of a poodle after all, and a poodle who had just seen a squirrel.

He walks to the exit and leave. Upon leaving the room, there is no option. He must go left.

Turn to **53**

23

Another long corridor stretches ahead, but eventually it comes to an end at a T-junction. To the left, the corridor goes underground into a dark earth lined tunnel. To the right, another bookshelf-lined stretch of corridor is evident.

If you want Mr. March to go down the tunnel, turn to **66**
If you want him to take the corridor to the right, turn to **50**

24

The left turn takes Mr. March to a stout oak door, with a brass plaque saying "*The Archives Room*"

Mr. March shrugs and opens the door to find a small room, with three walls lined with bookcases. The other wall opposite the door is a large inglenook fireplace and around this are a table and three wingback leather armchairs. A pleasant fire burns in the hearth, and on the table is a china tea service on a silver tray. In a blue and white cup is a still steaming-hot cup of tea - and yet no-one is around.

Frustrated, Mr. March sits down and picks up the tea and sips it. It's a bit too sweet for his liking, but still he drains the cup.
On the table is a large, black, leather bound book. There is just a large "*A*" embossed on the cover in gold leaf.

He opens the book, and the title page says:
"A History of The Archives by J. Crinkles , C. Holland and F. Ranter, first published 1888"

If you want Mr. March to read the book, turn to **9**
If you would rather he left the room, turn to **12**

25

Soon, a left turn appears, but the route also carries on straight ahead.

If you want Mr. March to turn left, turn to **60**
Otherwise he carries on going straight ahead, turn to **36**

26

Mr. March has started to feel very hungry. Mr. March likes his food, and eats almost constantly, and he gets irritated when he's hungry.

In fact there are only two things in the world that normally irritate Mr. March. Being lost, and being hungry. As he was currently both, he was very irritated. About as irritated as a nest of wasps spinning around in a concrete mixer.

To his right there is a short flight of steps down, or the corridor continues in front of him.

To go down the steps, turn to **56**
To go straight on, turn to **23**

27

Mr. March follows another corridor, which turns first to the left, and then to the left (again!). At the end of this, there is a T-junction, and Mr. March can either turn left or right.

For Mr. March to turn left, turn to **3**
For him to turn right, turn to **64**

28

Mr. March finds himself in a section of the Archives with a wooden plaque on the wall, saying "***Spores, molds and fungus***" ahead of him. Underneath is a carved picture of a mushroom

Mr. March can either head straight on, turn to **3**
Or he can turn left, turn to **20**

29

Once again another T-junction. If you want Mr. March:
To go left, turn to **11**
To turn right, turn to **7**

30

The long corridor head straight on for some time. It ends with two doors, one on the left, and one on the right. Both look identical

If you want Mr. March to take the left door, turn to **65**
If you want him to take the right door, turn to **75**

31

Mr. March pulls the book called "***Resolution***" out of the box. As he does so, the bookcase to his left slides to one side to reveal a doorway. Mr. March walks through it, and finds himself in a corridor (what a surprise!). The bookcase slams shut behind him.

Turn to **48**

32

Mr. March turns the corner and finds himself in a dead end, with more shelves facing him. A metal sign is screwed onto the wall above the shelf straight ahead of him. It says:

"Metals and ores"

There's a table and a chair in the cul-de-sac and on the table is a single book. It has a shiny metallic cover and on the front are just the letters "***AR***"

He can either turn and leave straight away, turn to **17**
Pick up the book from the table, turn to **13**

33

The corridor goes right, then left, then right again. Mr. March finds himself with another choice. A long dark corridor disappears off to his left, and to his right a ladder is bolted to the wall. Another corridor also stretches off in front.

Should Mr. March?
Go left? Turn to **43**
Climb the ladder? Turn to **69**
Go straight on? Turn to **26**

34

The corridor seems to go on forever, twisting and turning, and Mr. March is getting increasingly frustrated at not finding his way out.

Eventually, he arrives at a left turn, whereas ahead there just seems to be another bookcase in an alcove. On the wall above the bookcase is a wooden sign saying *"**Theatre Studies**"* and in smaller writing *"**On Loan from the Asian Archive**"*

If you want Mr. March to turn left, turn to **48**
If you want him to look at the bookcase, turn to **47**

35

Mr. March walks along between two tall stacks of books for about 100 metres, and then finds himself at another dead end. In front of him is a single bookshelf. It's empty apart from two books.

The book on the left is called "***A shortcut to mushrooms***"
The book on the right is called "***Up in smoke***"

If you want to Mr. March to pick up the left hand book, turn to **2**
If you want him to pick up the right hand book, turn to **4**

36

The corridor coils around like a snake in a circle, until Mr. March finds himself at another junction.

He can turn left, turn to **73**
Or go right, turn to **50**

37

Back on a main corridor, still lined with books on both sides, Mr. March carries on walking. Soon he arrives at a crossroads, with passages to the left, right and straight on.

If you want Mr. March to go left, turn to **27**
To go right, turn to **19**
For Mr. March to head straight on, turn to **34**

38

The corridor dog legs around to the left and then the right, before Mr. March finds himself at a dead end. Mr. March curses to himself under his breath. In front of him are three book shelves, piled high with books, one facing him, and the other two facing each other.

There's a sign on the wall behind, saying "***Ancient History***"

He was about to turn around and leave when he notices a book on one of the shelves. It had a dark red cover, the colour of dried blood, and was half poking out from the shelf as if it had been recently read. Curiously, Mr. March picks up the book. There was a slip of paper between two pages, acting as a bookmark. He turns to that page. It reads:

"In years gone by, the Gods of War have changed over time, depending on the state of human society and the way they waged war. When the human race first started to use tools and settle down into tribes, then the weapons they used were very basic.

Spears made of shafts of fire hardened wood, with heads of sharp flint spliced to the ends. Clubs made of shaped, thicker branches. Knives made of long pieces of sharp flint. Initially war between tribes was ugly, and up close, with lots of people whacking each other over the head.

But then one day someone took a long lean stick of ash, and tied a string made from the tendons from an animal between the ends, causing the stick to form a bow shape. Then they took a slim yard long stick, and put feathers on one end, and a small sharp point of stone on the other end.

The invention of the bow and arrow revolutionized both hunting and war, as prey and enemies could now be killed over a greater distance. A better food supply made humans stronger and bigger, and helped their brains and muscles to grow due to the protein heavy diet of meat, supplemented with nuts and berries.

During this time, the human race idolized the Gods of Wood and Stone. Small idols made of bundles of sticks, or pieces of stone, where made and worshipped. They carved huge stone faces, and erected temples of tall stones formed in a circle, and with an inner circle of tall trees.

Humans emerged from caves and built small villages made of houses of stone and wood, and protected themselves with tall fences of wood.

Even the act of burning wood in a stone firepit was seen as an act of worship – as fire made the food taste better, kept them warm and warded off predators. So the burning of wood was seen as a holy act – and anyway, if you snapped a branch from a tree, then the tree would grow again.

During this time, as they were worshipped across the human world, the gods of Wood and Stone were powerful beyond belief. They often walked the earth in human form. The God of Wood was small and slender, quick and clever. The God of Stone was tall and broad, and moved in the exact same way a mountain doesn't.

They reveled in this worship, and lived as they wished, and took what they wanted. They were not kind Gods. They provoked wars between tribes, as every death by wood or stone they saw as a sacrifice and it made them stronger. The time was known as the Age of Wood and Stone, although over time for some reason, Wood was forgotten about.

And then one day, about 3,000 years ago, some smart human found they could melt shiny ores found in the earth and mix them. These ores, copper and tin, would then harden to form a burnished, hard metal which they called bronze.

Soon the first sword was made of bronze, as were other tools, and although bows and arrows were still used, the arrows now had bronze tips, and the humans quickly forgot about their old gods.

Without the worship of the human population to feed their strength, then the Gods of Wood and Stone grew weaker and weaker.

They were trapped in their human form, although not exactly human as they were still made of wood and stone. They were powerful compared to a human, but no longer had god-like powers, more like supernatural powers.

They fell into despair, having no point to their life, but doomed to be immortal and have no meaning.

Then one day, a woman appeared before them in a flash of light seemingly from the stars. The woman was tall and slender, and was dressed in a brilliant white robe that shined incandescently. Her face was smooth and ageless, and she had long white hair.

"Gentlemen, can I have a word? You seem to be at a bit of a loss. I have a proposition for you." she said, charmingly.

The chapter ended, and Mr. March slammed the book closed and placed in back on the shelf.

"Well, that explains a few things" he said to himself, turning to leave the cul-de-sac.

Turn to **18**

39

Mr. March sets off along a twisting corridor, lined with books and bookcases on both sides. Eventually he gets to a crossroads.

Do you want Mr. March to?
Go left, turn to **67**
Carry on going straight on, turn to **42**
Go right, turn to **33**

40

The toadstool tastes almost woody as Mr. March gulps it down in three bites. Then he feels a strange sensation, as if he's feeling dizzy, and the room around him starts to feel like its fading away.

Then the room does actually fade away, and in front of Mr. March are two doors. On the left there is a green door. On the right is a red door.

Which door will Mr. March choose?
If you want him to take the green door, turn to **72**
If you want him to take the red door, turn to **63**

41

The problem with The Archive is that most the corridors seem to be the same. Each side is lined with shelves rammed full of books. But eventually there is a choice, as there is a side passage that snakes off to the right.

To go straight on with Mr. March, turn to **38**
To turn right, turn to **35**

42

Mr. March is faced with a long, straight, flight of metal steps that go slowly downwards as the corridor heads off into darkness. He places his left foot on the first step, then his right on the second.

As soon as both feet are on the steps, the top of all the steps angles down with a click, so that the stairs now form a steep metal slide.

Mr. March's feet go from under him, and he slips and slithers down the slippery slide. He then sees ahead of him that he is heading for a wall. He puts his hands in front of him, and braces for impact. But before he hits the wall, the floor underneath him drops down, into a very steep slide and he drops down into darkness. He lands at the bottom with a "*thud*". He hauls himself to his feet and shrugs. Nothing surprises him about this infernal place anymore.

In front of him is a door to the left, and a corridor heading straight on.

For Mr. March to go through the door, turn to **22**
If you want him to go straight on, turn to **53**

43

The route now branches off, with one part going diagonally off to the left, and the other to the right. Which route should Mr. March take?
To go left, turn to **19**
To go right, turn to **33**

44

After another hundred yards, there is a further turning and another decision to be made. Do you want Mr. March to:

Go straight on, turn to **37**
Turn right, turn to **32**

45

Mr. March is glad to be out of the dank and dark woods, and return to a more normal part of The Archives. Ahead of you is the way he came, and so Mr. March decides to turn right.

Turn to **20**

46

The corridor turns into a tunnel that is lined with mud and earth. It's incredibly dark and musty and carries on and on. Mr. March is not particularly happy underground and turns round unsure – and then he notices a small door, only 3 feet high, in the wall of the tunnel.

If you want Mr. March to carry on down the tunnel, turn to **66**
If you want him to crawl through the door, turn to **51**

47

Mr. March looks closely at the bookcase, looking at a few books and inspecting them but seeing nothing unusual.

There are three books in a box set together that then catch Mr. Marchs' eye. He picks up the box set and looks at it.

The books in the set are called: "***Character***", "***Conflict***" and "***Resolution***"

To take out the book called "***Character***", turn to **10**
To take out the book called "***Conflict***", turn to **15**
To take out the book called "***Resolution***", turn to **31**

48

Mr. March strolls down the corridor, which is quite short and soon ends in a T-junction. To the left, the corridor goes underground into a dark earth-lined tunnel. To the right, another bookshelf lined stretch of corridor is evident.

Mr. March can now:
Turn left, turn to **46**
Turn right, turn to **50**

49

Mr. March is back in the twisting corridor
"This whole place is twisted" he thinks to himself, grumpily.

Do you want Mr. March to?
Turn left, turn to **42**
Carry on going straight on, turn to **33**

50

There's a short walk unto there is a door on the left wall.

If you want Mr. March to go through the door, turn to **74**
If you just want him to carry on, turn to **58**

51

Mr. March tugs the door open and sees a small passageway, only 3 foot tall, on the other side. Shrugging, he crawls through the doorway and along the passage.

He's quite happy on all fours, but he has to stop himself when he gets an urge to cock his leg and relieve himself. Being back on all fours brings him closer to his wolfish side. He fights an urge to wag his tail, as at the moment he has no tail and he would just end up wiggling his bum. Which would look ridiculous.

He crawls on and the passage slowly gets taller, and soon he is back on two legs. Ahead of him is a doorway, to his right is a long straight corridor.

To go through the door, turn to **22**
To go right up the corridor, turn to **53**

52

Straight on, there's a doorway ahead of Mr. March, and on the door is a silver plaque, saying:

"Unnatural History"

Mr. March opens the door and goes through. On the other side is a laboratory. There are jars with specimens of various creatures stored in them. Here there is a jar labelled "were-bat" and in the clear jar, a very furry bat with huge pointed teeth is suspended in a yellowy liquid. Elsewhere in a tall thin jar, a bit like one your parents may use to store spaghetti, is seemingly empty. But the label simply said *"poltergeist"*. As Mr. March stared into the jar, he could see a faint white form swirling around in the jar.

In the corner of the room is a human skeleton. At least Mr. March thinks it's a human skeleton, but then he goes closer. The skeleton is taller and thinner than a human, with an elongated skull with a huge cranium. The arms are inordinately long, with the middle finger much longer than the others. In the skull, there are only two teeth in the top jawbone - two long sharp pointed fangs.

As Mr. March peers at the skull, it turns to look at him (a neat trick when you have no eyes) and the jaw opens and closes a few times, making a clackedly clack sound. Mr. March jumps back in alarm.

Recovering his poise, he walks over to one of the tall desks and notices a huge leather journal on it. He opens it and looks inside, about halfway through, and sees:

"Experiment 1823/3, date 2 December 2020
It has long been known that vampyrs are able to sleep for a long time when they choose, to get through difficult times in history. When a vampyr starts a long sleep, then its body almost totally shuts down. It does not need blood to survive, although it gets weaker the longer it slumbers.

This specimen was last seen at 8am on 2 Sept 2020. It went into a long sleep, or hibernation, as the sun rose. By monitoring its brainwaves we were able to find out the below.

As the vampyr sleeps during the day, it is oblivious to all around it. This is consistent with both vampyrs in a daily sleep cycle, and those in a long sleep.

However, when the vampyr is in a long sleep, then when the sun goes down, the vampyrs brain wakes up. It is not fully conscious, but we were able to see that the cochleae nerves of the ears of the vampyr were very active. They seemed to take information coming in from the outside world.

Vampyrs are linked, unnaturally, to bats (hence they can take their form)……

("Ha" laughed Mr. March, normally they can", remembering Chillingworth as a rather shocked green squirrel.)

"…..and have a highly developed sense of hearing. And ridiculously big ears, which makes wearing a hat very difficult. As they lie asleep at night, their ears can hear what is going on around them for a half a mile radius.

It seems that there is a practical reason for this. It means as they hibernate, they can still take in what's happening around them.

This means that if they wake up after 20 years asleep, they still have some knowledge about the modern world – so as to try to fit in (as well as a creature with huge pointy ears, two long fangs and a thirst for blood can fit in).

They would also get advanced notice if the council had decided to build a bypass through their house – and so they could wake up and move, instead of being dug up by a JCB. Which would do little or no damage to them (or the JCB) but be very inconvenient.

Previously, in quieter days, they would soak up the information from houses nearby, and get to know the local residents and their lives.

However, since the prevalence of TV, radio, and mobile phones, then these days they tend to soak up a lot of information as they sleep at night and people are sat in front of the TV. Therefore when then awake they are unlikely to know who the President of Uganda is, but they will probably know if Ian Beale and Phil Mitchell are having another feud in EastEnders.

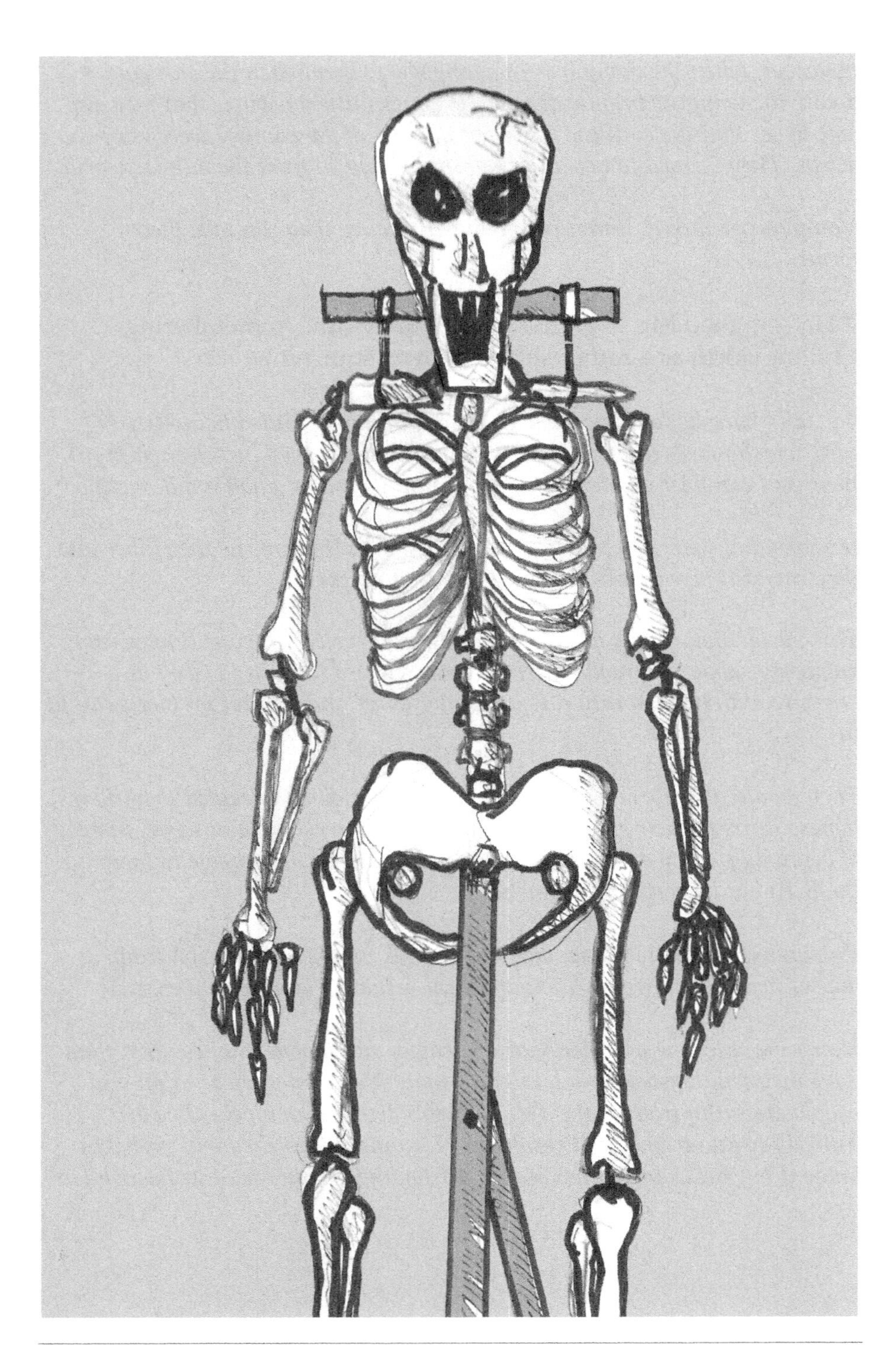

They also tend to hear a lot of popular music from radio broadcasts, which means they would be a valuable addition to a quiz team for Wednesday night's pop quiz at the Frog and Parrot (free entry, chips and gravy at half time, jackpot round, all welcome). Well, they would be if they didn't have the tendency to drink their team-mates.

The upshot of this is that when a vampyr does awaken after a long sleep, its knowledge of the current world will be patchy, and depend upon if their neighbors like watching Transformers movies or Ru Paul's Drag Race. However for some reason, they can't seem to receive any 5G phone networks"

The report carried on, but as usual Mr. March had lost interest. He stared once more at the skeleton, which seemed to smile at him with a toothy grin, and then he (Mr. March, not the skeleton) turned and left the room.

He decided to go left as he left. Turn to **7**

53

Mr. March soon arrives at another crossroad. Will he:
Go left, turn to **50**
Go straight on, turn to **63**
Go right, turn to **73**

54

Don't leave me this way.

55

The corridor goes right, then left, then right again. Mr. March finds himself with another choice. A long dark corridor disappears off to his right, and next to him is a ladder that is bolted to the wall. Another corridor also stretches off to the left.

Should Mr. March?
Climb the ladder? Turn to **69**
Go left, turn to **26**
Go right, turn to **71**

56

The stone stairs take Mr. March down into a dark, damp, dank cellar. The ceiling is low and arched, so that he has to stoop over as he walks through it. On both sides are large oak barrels. Further along, the cellar opens into a small room, with a single desk and chair. On the desk is a newspaper, bowl of fruit, a bottle of wine and a crystal glass.

Seeing only the food and drink, Mr. March sits down at the desk and grabs an apple and wolfs it down - literally as he is part wolf. He spits out the pips, as apple pips aren't good for wolves (or dogs). He then grabs a pear, and devours it at the same speed. He slows down a bit as he decides it's probably best to peel the tangerines and bananas. Whilst he is doing this he pops the cork out of the bottle and pours himself a glass of red wine.

After he has peeled the tangerines, he eats them segment by segment, sipping the wine, feeling a lot happier now he isn't as hungry. Now he is only lost.

His eyes fall onto the front page of the newspaper. When I say fall onto the paper, they don't drop out of his head with a plop. He just looks down.

ARCHIVE GAZETTE

EUROPEAN DAILY EDITION

Issue No. 1,432,591 Editor: C. Holland since 1852 Published: Tomorrow

Mr. Sticks snapped and Mr. Stones smashed

Well known paranormal thugs for hire Mr. Sticks and Mr. Stones have been brought down to size by three children and a scruffy werewolf. When asked for comment, Mr. Sticks, who was still re-attaching his arms, refused to reply (or couldn't answer the phone). Mr. Stones is understood to be pursuing a new career as a garden ornament.

ATLANTEAN OPEN DAY

The floating, mostly submerged, continent of Atlantis if planning on rising off the coast of Southern Ireland this Freyersday.

The Archives will be opening their doors for the afternoon to allow anyone to visit.. If you are visiting, please try not to get lost. Cont.,.,p2

LAIRS, SECRET HQ's and **DENS** for **HIRE**! Call 666-616-6666-6

Missing!

Have you seen this man / wolf?

Last seen in The European Archives on Tiwesday. Please feed if found.

ANTARCTICA-DABRA

A day in the Life of the Antarctic Archives.

Situated in Port Lockroy on Wiencke Island, the Archives that hold all the literature on magic, magicians and magical items. The Archive is situated just off a remote, beautiful and, often very, cold peninsular.

The Archivist, Jerimiah Crinkles, who has been in charge since 1892, is a short, squat man with thick dark hair and a thin dark moustache.. Continued Page 5…………..

Births, Death and Marriages:

Births: None Deaths: None Marriages: None

CRICKET

Day 56 of the Inter-Archive test will continue on Wodensday, with Franciois Ranter resuming on 1,745 not out, after an innings of 11 days. This takes the North American Archive to a score of 24,345 / 121. …………………Continued back page

Films and TV

Shadow Thief: The Movie,

Rating: ★★★★★

Director: D Gillson, Release date: Thorsday .

See full review on Page 13

I

t's entitled the Archive Gazette (Europe edition), and rather oddly it's dated with tomorrows date. He flicks through it, seeing tomorrow's football results, yesterday's weather, and last week's horrorscopes. The horrorscopes are particularly gruesome. Then he turns to the adverts.

He skims through them, until he stops at a small advert near the bottom of the left page. It says:

NOW HIRING.
EVER THOUGHT ABOUT A CAREER AS A HENCH-MAN / HENCH-WOMAN / HENCH-CREATURE?

DUE TO RECENT FORCED REDUNDANCIES, WE ARE HIRING.

EVER WANTED TO MURDER, MAIM AND CAUSE MAYHEM?

EVER WANTED TO ERADICATE, ELIMINATE AND EXTERMINATE?

THEN WHY NOT GET PAID DOING SO?

GOOD RATES OF PAY, GOOD HOURS, AND EXCELLENT PENSION SCHEME. REQUIREMENTS TO WORK DAY AND NIGHT, AND WEEKENDS*

**FLEXIBLE WORKING AVAILABLE FOR VAMPYRS, LYCAN AND ANYONE ELSE SENSITIVE TO SUNLIGHT*

CONTACT MISS WORDS BY:
LOOKING INTO AN UPSIDE DOWN SILVER MIRROR, AND SAYING MY NAME BACKWARDS FIVE TIMES

MISS WORDS, AN EQUAL OPPORTUNITIES EMPLOYER SINCE THE BRONZE AGE

"Hmmm" thinks Mr. March to himself, "It seems the maybe Mr. Sticks and Mr. Stones are no longer gainfully employed".

He grins, wolfishly, finishes his last segment of tangerine and gulp of wine, pops the bananas in his pocket for later, and leaves the cellar.

Turn to **23**

57

The door creeps open and it's quite a small room, with only one bookshelf. Mr. March wanders through the door and picks up the first book on the shelf. It's entitled:

"The Long Term Effects of Remaining in the same form measured over time and space for different amimorphic creatures; a longitudinal study set over experimental conditions to establish and, if possible, illustrate the benefits and drawbacks of remaining in an altered state for an extended period of time"

The title is so long Mr. March almost falls asleep on his feet just from reading it. It's also so long it won't all fit on the spine of the (rather slim) book, and so someone has written it in pen the rest of the title on the back of the book.

However, as an animorph, he decides to have a look. An anamorph is a being who can turn, or is turned, into another physical form. His anamorphic form is as a great wolf. Sir Francis' animorphs are when he turned into a bat or a mischief of rats - at least they used to be.

Mr. March flicks open the book and wishes he hadn't. There are lots of tables that tabulate the data from the charts, and charts that illustrate the content of the tables.

Mr. March detests charts with a passion and finds tables tedious to the extreme. Spreadsheets are an anathema to him, and databases drive him to distraction. But he eventually turns to a page entitled "***Conclusion***". He has a quick read of one of the paragraphs,

"Our key findings are that when an animorph changes from his primary form; which is normally humanoid, into their secondary form; normally animal, then the longer the time spent in their secondary form, the harder the change back proves to be; and in fact it may eventually prove to be impossible, or at least highly improbable."

"For Pete's sake, why don't academics like full stops?" thought Mr. March to himself. He was mentally exhausted from getting to the end of such a long sentence, so much so that he forgot what the start of the sentence meant. He thought about re-reading it but really couldn't face it. But gallantly, he continued reading,

"In summary, the longer the humanoid is in their secondary animalistic form, then the more the animal side of their nature expands and the humanoid side diminishes. If a humanoid does not, or cannot, change back to humanoid within a set period of time, then they lose the desire (and in some cases the ability) to turn back to humanoid. However, if the humanoid form of the anamorph has an extended life, then if trapped in animal form, they will still retain this."

"Hmm, interesting" mused Mr. March, "I wonder what effect this will have on the Professor, and his current incarceration. Maybe Flora will get a pet squirrel after all."

He grinned at the thought, thinking how apt it would be for Chillingworth to become immortal after all, but end up as an immortal green squirrel.

This all gave him a warm fuzzy feeling, and he slid the book back on the shelf and left the room, feeling a lot happier than he had for some time.

As he leaves, he turns to his right. Turn to **73**

58

The corridor zigs then zags, and then zags and zig, and then goes back to zagging again.

"It really can't make up its mind" muttered Mr. March under its breath.

But eventually, there is a left turn, or a door straight ahead. On a plaque on the door is inscribed the words "***Amimorphics***"

If you want Mr. March to go through the door, turn to **57**
If you want him to turn left, turn to **73**

59

Mr. March is sure he has been here before as he finds himself in another book lined corridor. But that's no great surprise. He promised to never again complain about being dragged around IKEA by Mrs. Bannerworth when she needed some new tea lights and an occasional table.

And what's the deal with occasional table?, he mused. It never changes form so surely it's a permanent table.

Turn to **7**

60

Soon Mr. March finds himself in a corridor that ends with a crossroads.

"Please be the final crossroads" pleads Mr. March to himself. "If its not, I will be livid"

He can go left, turn to **11**
He can go straight on, turn to **62**
To go right, turn to **36**

61

CONGRATULATIONS!

You have managed to help Mr. March find Mr. H., and he is no longer Lost in The Archives.

If you enjoyed this adventure, then there are a whole world of gamebooks out there you could try. Please see the end of the book for some recommendations.

62

The corridor turns to the right and soon there is a door in front of Mr. March. It's a wonky door.

If you want him to go through the door, turn to **68**

Otherwise you can follow the road around, turn to **59**

63

Mr. March pulls open the red door and walks through it. He feels a kind of spinning sensation as if the world around him is changing, which is pretty accurate, as it is. He finds himself in a corridor.

The corridor seems to go on forever, twisting and turning, and Mr. March is getting increasingly frustrated at not finding his way out.

Eventually, he arrives at a left turn, whereas ahead there just seems to be another bookcase in an alcove. On the wall above the bookcase is a wooden sign saying "***Theatre Studies***" and in smaller writing "***On Loan from the Asian Archive***"

If you want Mr. March to turn left, turn to **48**
If you want him to look at the bookcase, turn to **47**

64

Another junction! The choices are to go left or right.
To go left with Mr. March, turn to **44**;
To go right, turn to **38**

65

You step through the door and find yourself in a comfortable chamber, like a study. There's a desk straight ahead of you with a reading lamp. Behind the desk is Mr. H, his head deep in a book. He looks up and smiles pleasantly.

"Ah, Mr. M, is it Wodensday already? Time for our weekly game?"

Mr. March bristled a bit, still a bit shaken up from his ordeal in The Archives.

"Wodensday, no, Mr. H, we were researching somewhere in The Archives on Thorsday morning, and you left to go and find something to aid the search. But you never came back. I have been looking for you ever since"

Usually a very relaxed and easy going person, Mr. March had been shaken up by his experience, and was struggling to stay calm. The fact he was still really hungry didn't help.

"Oh my word, were we?" replied Mr. H, "My sincere apologies, my good man, I got distracted. When was that?"

He looked at a desk calendar in front of him, which automatically changed each day - which was just as well as Mr. H would never remember to change it.

"Goodness, its Saturnsday now. It seems you have been lost for some time"

"Saturnsday? I've been in that place for 2 days?" Mr. March nearly shouted, but didn't.

"So it appear, my dear Mr. M. Deary dreary me, you must be starving"

"Ravenous"

"Well then, let me make amends and prepare a banquet for you. Wait here, and I will return shortly". Mr. H stood on and headed for the door.

"Oh, no you don't, Mr. H, I'm not letting you out of my sight again in this infernal place!" Mr. March replied, flustered at the thought of being left alone, again.

"Very well, then Mr. M. Follow me and we will make our way to the kitchens"

Relieved, Mr. March follows Mr. H out of the study, back into a book lined corridor.

"And whilst I remember, Mr. H, I've got a few questions to ask you. How come I never get lost anywhere, but I always get lost here. There must be a reason?"

"Ah, Mr. H, that's complicated, you see, what happens is................"

Turn to **61**

66

Down into the dank earth Mr. March goes, into a tunnel that's almost pitch black even to Mr. March's miraculous eyesight. He feels his way along the tunnel, seemingly for hours, but in reality it's only a few minutes. Then he sees a circle of light ahead of him and the tunnel starts to rise upwards.

Mr. March clambers up the steep incline of the tunnel, and out into the fresh air. Well, fresh compared to the tunnel. Once again he is in another part of The Archives. There are two options:

He can go straight on, turn to **52**
Or he can go right, turn to **7**

67

The left turn ends up in a little snug like room with no other exits. There is a table with a lamp, and a chair next to it. There are also a pile of books on the floor, next to the chair, but little else. The top book grabs Mr. March's attention - which is normally a tricky thing to do. It's called,

"Of Humans, Wolves and other Animals: a study into Lycanthropy"

Interested, Mr. March sits down and picks up the book and turns to a random page and starts reading.

"Lycanthropes are creatures who spend most of their lives in a human form, but at certain times transform into other creatures, normally animals with anthropomorphic properties.

Best known are werewolves, where a human turns into a wolf during nights when the moon is full. This is mainly due to their prevalence in modern fiction and cinema. Contrary to their appearance in horror films and penny dreadfuls, werewolves aren't particularly violent or aggressive, and are more like an oversized dog – and they are about as clever when they are in wolf form as a golden retriever"

Mr. March felt vaguely insulted by that. Most golden retrievers he had met were as thick as stuffing. But he read on.

"They can be friendly and faithful, and will normally only attack if someone threatens them or their friends, who they see as part of their pack. They often adopt another human, or paranormal entity, as a dog would a human. They can be a danger to livestock though.

Also, modern fiction is incorrect in stating that they can only turn into a wolf at a full moon. They can in fact turn at any time, but normally only when their human self is very emotional – so very angry or upset, or someone they care for is in danger.

If they change under these conditions, they can be very dangerous to anyone who they perceive to have threatened them or their pack"

Mr. March smiled to himself at reading that, as he vaguely remembered the game of fetch he and Henry had with Mr. Stick's limbs. He carried on reading

"When in their animal form, lycanthropes have little of their human memories and act a lot more out of instinct. When they return to human form they remember little of their time in their other form"

"Too true" thought Mr. March. Early in his days as a lycan, there had been some terribly embarrassing incidents when he woke up naked the next day: In a shop window, in the beer garden of a pub, or on the 8:15 to Waterloo.

"As well as were-wolves, there are also many other types of lycanthropes. They include were-bats, were-rats, were-gerbils, and were-rabbits, but none of these seem to warrant a horror film as they are not particularly scary. In fact the biggest danger concerning a were-rat is towards the rat itself, as they often get eaten by an were-owl. And a were-rabbit will not cause you any harm, unless you are trying to grow prize vegetables in the garden.

Were-beasts are harder to kill than most animals and humans, and can quickly recover from injury and sometimes even re-grow limbs.

Silver bullets don't hurt them. Or rather they do, but because they are bullets, not because they are made of silver. And bullets are supposed to hurt.

The only affect silver has on a lycan is that it can stop the human changing into their other form, as the silver catches and stores the beams from the moon."

"Well, none of that is hardly anything new to me" grumbled Mr. March, slamming the book closed. But even so, he popped the book into his jacket pocket so he could read it later - mainly just to check for accuracies so he could write to the author and tell them. If he remembered. Which he probably wouldn't.

With that he left the snug.

Turn to **49**

68

Behind the wonky door is a small room. It seems to be a study with a single desk and chair. A quill pen and ink are on the desk, as well as a long vellum parchment. Mr. March walks over and looks at the parchment, and reads the title

"A dissertation into the governance of the natural and supernatural world"

The opening paragraph reads:
"One of the bigger questions of recent decades has been who runs the world. Most mortals tend to think that they do, or no one does. Those that think that someone does also tend to think that that someone should be sacked for doing such a rubbish job.

Vampyrs like to think they rule the mortal and supernatural world, but in reality they don't rule anything. Getting a groups of vampyrs to work together is a bit like herding a clutter of were-cats.

The problem is, the older vampyrs get, the bigger their egos get, and so they always think they are the cleverest person (or being) in the room – even when with any other vampyrs. Also, being immortal means that little matters that mortals decide on quickly take forever for vampyrs to make a decision on.

It once took the vampyr council 5 years and 13,356 rounds of voting to decide who was going out to get new candles for the council chamber. In the end no one did and they all ended up sat in the dark until someone thought to call the electricity company and get some lights installed (that took another 2 years).

In fact, the most common thing they argue about is whether they are called "The Vampyr Council", or "The Council of Vampyrs". The argument has been raging for two thousand years and still no one can decide.

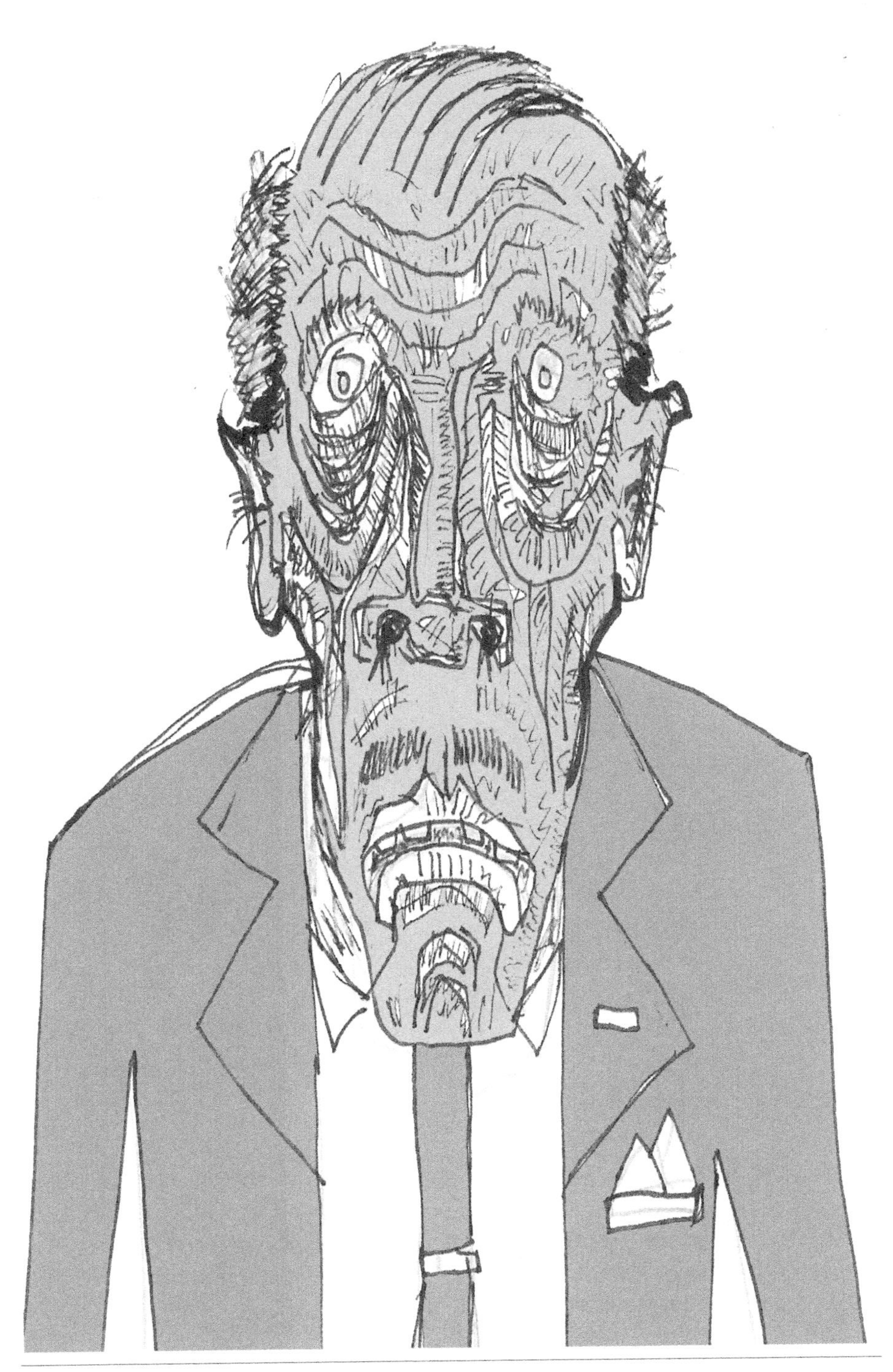

Zombies aren't normally known for their intelligence, and they definitely don't run the world but they do tend to control a lot of the money. Zombies can mostly pass as human, most of the time, but their natures tend to be that they are slow, single minded and persistent. This means they tend to be drawn towards jobs that require high levels of tedium and boredom – which is why they tend to become chartered accountants or financial analysts.

A recent poll in "Undead Life" magazine found that 77% of accountancy firms were run by zombies – which is quite believable if you ever try to have a conversation with an accountant. Or an interesting conversation.

Were-creatures don't really care who runs the world. Were-wolves are happy as long as they get a scratch behind the ear, a bone to chew on and a ball to chase. Were-wolves love chasing balls, which is probably why a surprising amount of professional footballers are were-wolves (it's normally the really hairy ones)."

Mr. March felt a bit upset by that, but he carried on reading,

"It's similar with were-gerbils. They have a great affinity for running endlessly on wheels, which is why a lot of them, when in human form, work at the fairs on the walzers or the big wheel."

Mr. March nodded. Were-gerbils were obsessed with wheels.

"Djinn (rhymes with gin), or Genies as they are more commonly known, have little interest in the mortal world, apart from when they need to escape from bottles or lamps. Ghosts and spectres......."

Mr. March got bored and stop reading.

He looked up and noticed that there was another door, mostly hidden by a curtain, at the other side of the room.

If you want Mr. March to leave by the door he came in through, then turn to **60**
If you want him to leave by the new door, turn to **11**

69

Mr. March quickly climbs up the ladder, and finds a hatch in the ceiling above it. He pushes it open and pulls himself up into the space with his strong, lanky arms.

It's a dark and dingy attic space. There's hardly any light, but Mr. March doesn't need much light to see by. He looks around. Dust is all over the floor, and there are pieces of furniture that are covered with white dust sheets. The dust is inches thick on the floor – as if no one has been up here in decades, or maybe centuries.

Mr. March walks around, sneezing slightly due to the dust he is kicking up into the air. Mr. March has a very sensitive nose. He really hates walking past those posh soap shops (rhymes with "Mush") in town as they always make him sneeze and give him a headache.

Further along are a series of portraits on the wall, cobwebs hanging from them. Picking up a scrap of material from a covered desk, he rubs the dust away from the first one. And sneezes again. It's a portrait of a pretty young woman in a yellow dress. There's a name plaque underneath it, saying:

"Cordelia Holland, 1782"

The next two pictures are landscapes, of where it is not clear - although in one the sky is green and the grass is blue, which is a tad unusual. Then he checks the final picture and finds another portrait, this time of an old man. Mr. March stops dead after he wipes the dust from the portrait.

The old man has the same eyes, the same nose, even the same pinched look about his face as Mr. Holland. Everything, the bone structure, the hair, is identical to Mr. H, apart from the age.

He wipes the dust off the name plaque, and sees the name:

"Charles Holland, 1672"

He knew Mr. H was old, older than most humans ever dream of being, but he had never asked his age. He's reminded of a book by Oscar Wilde, where a man stays young whilst a painting of him ages. Mr. March hadn't read the book. Trying to get Mr. March to read a whole book is a bit like trying to get a spaniel to do algebra. It's never going to happen. However he did see the film with Angela Lansbury at the cinema when it came out.

More than a little rattled, he stares once more at the painting, which seems to stare back at him, and then turns.

He walks back to the hatch, and down the ladder, away from the dusty attic, sneezing once more.

Another thing to ask Mr. Holland - if he ever actually finds him.

Back on the ground, Mr. March can now:
Go to the left, turn to **39**
Go straight on, turn to **43**
Go right, turn to **26**

70

Soon Mr. March finds himself in a corridor that ends with a crossroads.

"Please be the final crossroads" pleads Mr. March to himself.

He can go right, turn to **11**
He can go straight on, turn to **59**
To go left, turn to **36**

71

Mr. March sets off along a twisting corridor, lined with books and bookcases on both sides. Eventually he gets to a crossroads. His heart sinks, as he sees that straight ahead is the cul-de-sac he started in.

Cursing under his breath, he has to make a choice. Will he:
Go straight on, turn to **67**
Go right, turn to **42**

72

Mr. March pulls open the green door and walks through it. He feels a kind of spinning sensation as if the world around him is changing, and then he finds himself in a corridor that zigs then zags, and then zags and zig, and then goes back to zagging again.

"It really can't make up its mind" muttered Mr. March under his breath.

But eventually, there is a left turn, or a door straight ahead. On a plaque on the door is inscribed the words "***Amimorphics***"

If you want Mr. March to go through the door, turn to **57**
If you want him to turn left, turn to **73**

73

Mr. March strides along a corridor that somehow seems wonky. None of the shelves are straight. The roof seems to be higher at one side then the other, and then the other way around.
Eventually, he arrives at a wonky door ahead of him, or there is a small corridor off to the left.

If you want Mr. March to go through the door, turn to **68**
Otherwise he carries on down the corridor, turn to **60**

74

A sturdy oak door faces Mr. March, who pushes it open. Or rather he would have done if it wasn't for the fact the door needed to be pulled and so he walks into the door, and bruises his nose. Irritated, he grabs the door handle and pulls it open. He walks though and sees a large, grand room, with rows and rows of bookshelves. There's a sign on a stand, in polished bronze, and inscribed on it in elegant type are the words "***Undead politics***"

He randomly pulls a book from a shelf, entitled "***The A-Z of Undead Politics for Dummies***"

"Undead politics is complicated. It's not split down right wing and left wing like human politics. Undead politics never even gets that far. The greatest point of discussion over the last 150 years is over how they like to refer to themselves.

Beings that were mortal and turned into supernatural forms, such as vampyrs and zombies, have the most problem with this. In short, although in undead politics nothing is ever short, then there are several main factions:

Undead supporters, or dead-heads: these tend to be the traditional vampyrs and older zombies, who have always been known as undead and see no reason to change. But then the traditional vampyrs often see no reason to change their clothes and so they can be a bit stinky.

The Not-deads, or Notties: They believe that as they can still hear, smell, touch, taste, think etc. that they cannot be dead, and were never dead. The main reason this movement started was they were sick of being officially proclaimed as dead, and so losing their house, their money and their vinyl collection – which was inevitably sold on eBay by their nieces and nephews for a fraction of its true worth.

I'M NOT DEAD
I'M JUST BADLY
- DRAWN -
I DON'T CARE
BOO!
NOTTS
NOT-NOTTERS
UNDEAD
AND
LOVING
IT!
HONEST

The Not Dead, Not undead – Not-Nots: A splinter group of the Notties that formed their own party in 1982. They refuse to believe they were ever dead, and so cannot be undead, as this makes no sense. They will insists that they are not-dead and not-undead until they are blue in the face (which is quite common with vampyrs)

Transmortals – A relatively new faction which identify as all, but doesn't like labelling themselves. So they have labelled themselves as transmortals.

Ghosts and spectres are quite happy to be labelled as dead, as their physical bodies have long since gone, and so it's hard to argue that they aren't. But they don't really care anyway. They tend to be the happiest of the supernatural creatures, as all they are interested in is haunting houses. They are not evil or even malignant, but just normally mischievous spirits who get a childish delight in scaring the pants off poor mortals in the dead of night."

"Yep, ghosts are cool" thought Mr. March to himself and some of his best friends were ghouls.

But politics bores Mr. March, and so he leaves the room, first dropping the book on a nearby table.

As he leaves, he turns left. Turn to **58**

75

Mr. March goes through the door and finds himself in a cul-de-sac of bookshelves – of which there are many in The Archives. The same cul-de-sac he was in when Mr. H left him!

He walks out, and sees that the bookcases and shelves spread out in front of him, and to the left and the right.

He groans to himself when he realises he is going to have to start again!

Do you want Mr. March to?

Go left, turn to **5**

Go straight on, turn to **39**

Go right, turn 48

Quiz time!

A chance to win!

Below are 22 questions. The answers to all of them are to be found somewhere in The Archives. If you can successfully answer all 22 correct, then you may win a prize!

1. What was Dracula's original name?
2. What jobs do zombies like?
3. How many Archives are there?
4. What year did the Not-Nots start their party?
5. Who were once the Gods of War?
6. What would happen if a werewolf spends too long in wolf form?
7. What was the vampyr called who tried to work in movies?
8. On which train did Mr March wake up naked on?
9. What was the experiment number for the research into sleeping vampyrs?
10. What year was the portrait of Mr. H painted?
11. How many rounds of votes did it take before the Council of Vampyrs (or is it the Vampyrs' Council?) went out and got some new candles?
12. What is the metal "*Argent*" more commonly known as?
13. What are un-dead supporters also called?

14. Who was recruiting for Hench-men/ women / creatures?
15. What is another name for the creatures such as vampyrs and werewolves, who can change into animals?
16. What subject does the Atlantean Archive hold books on?
17. Who was in another portrait in the Archives?
18. What metallic alloy did humans discover that ended the Stone (and Wood!) age?
19. What is a group of rabbits called?
20. What was inside the seemingly tall, but empty, spaghetti jar?
21. How do you contact Miss Words?
22. Which dog is the average werewolf (in wolf form) about as clever as?

If you can answer them all, then please email your answers to: **Blackdoggamebooks@gmail.com**

Please include your name, age, and your favorite character in the book.

And you could win:

- A page of original art from the book
- An original sketch of your favourite character in Varney The Vampyr,
- A signed bookplate for the book, with a new image not in the book,
- A bookmark

Terms and conditions apply. Open only to UK residents. Entrants have to be 16 or under.

Who is Varney the Vampire

Varney the Vampire (not vampyr, rhymes with mere. Sorry), the Feast of Blood, was first published sometime between 1845 and 1847. It was serialised weekly in affordable pamphlets known as "Penny Dreadfuls". It was written by James Malcolm Rymer or Thomas Peckett Prest, or both of them.

Penny Dreadfuls cost, not surprisingly, a penny, and were typically 8-16 pages long and published each week. They are seen as being the first mass market produced stories for working class young men - and sold a million copies a week. Maybe they were the forerunner of modern comics. In fact, Marvel comics used the name Varnae for the first vampire ever in their universe - who came from the mythical city of Atlantis (before it sunk). But more of Atlantis later.

Penny Dreadfuls typically focused on supernatural beings, or detective stories. Other stories that were serialised as Penny Dreadfuls include Dick Turpin and Sweeney Todd, the Demon Barber of Fleet Street.

I first heard about Varney in the Stephen King book 'Salems Lot - and in fact Sir Francis' appearance is in part based on a character in the TV version of the book, made in 1979. Ask your parents before reading the book or watching the series, as it gave me sleepless nights and nightmares as a kid!

Varney was published more than 50 years before Bram Stokers Dracula, and Varney actually established a lot of the standard lore about vampires - for example it's the first book to give vampires pointed fang like teeth, hypnotic powers and superhuman strength.

It's very long and rambling (as the author got paid by the word), with 232 chapters, and about 667,000 words (the Lord of the Rings trilogy is "only" 481,103-ish words long). It's very inconsistent as the time its set, as well as the place, seems to change without reason. Plots start and never seem to finish and get forgotten about.

In the book, Sir Francis Varney torments the Bannerworth children, George, Flora and Henry, who live with their mother Mrs. Bannerworth, and their lodger, Mr. Marchdale. Other characters include Charles Holland, Floras uncle, and Jack Pringle. You should be familiar with all these names by now.

Varney is also seen as being the first sympathetic vampire, who hates his condition, but can do little to stop it.

Then Dracula came along in 1897 and took all the fame and glory, with his castle in the mountains, long capes, and dashing good looks.

I like to think that by bringing Sir Francis back to life (but was he ever dead?) then maybe a few more people will get to know about Sir Francis and appreciate the impact his story had on the myth of the vampire. And I have always thought it was quite a funny name for a vampire.

David Lowrie, 18th March 2021

Printed in Great Britain
by Amazon